"Is there no romance in that cool little soul of yours?"

Rio's blood was surging along her veins with an emotional mix of fear and excitement in response to Cameron's light kisses. "We're both supposed to be scientists," she answered, dry-mouthed.

"To be precise, we're both biologists." Then Cameron smiled. "And you seem remarkably blind to the biology evolving between us." He continued to kiss Rio's temples with great care, causing her to close her eyes with an involuntary shiver of response. "Which are you, Rio?" he murmured. "Unobservant—or willfully blind?"

"Nothing's evolving between us," Rio responded breathlessly. "And I find it odd that at a time like this you should be thinking of—of sex!"

"Willfully blind," he said softly, and slanted his head to kiss her with a force that took utter possession of her.

MADELEINE KER, one of our British authors, is a self-described "compulsive writer." In fact, Madeleine has been known to deliver six romances in less than a year. The author is married, and in addition to a writing career, is a graduate student at Durham University.

Books by Madeleine Ker

HARLEQUIN PRESENTS
642—AQUAMARINE
656—VIRTUOUS LADY
672—PACIFIC APHRODITE
699—THE WINGED LION
739—WORKING RELATIONSHIP
778—OUT OF THIS DARKNESS
795—FIRE OF THE GODS
884—DANGER ZONE
947—IMPACT

HARLEQUIN ROMANCE
2595—VOYAGE OF THE MISTRAL
2636—THE STREET OF THE FOUNTAIN
2709—ICE PRINCESS
2716—HOSTAGE

MADELEINE KER

frazer's law

Harlequin Books

TORONTO • NEW YORK • LONDON
AMSTERDAM • PARIS • SYDNEY • HAMBURG
STOCKHOLM • ATHENS • TOKYO • MILAN

Harlequin Presents first edition July 1988
ISBN 0-373-11090-1

Original hardcover edition published in 1987
by Mills & Boon Limited

CHAPTER ONE

THE dark shape flickered within the green glass wall of the wave that curled lazily over Rio; a big fish, big as a man, the proud dorsal fin clearly visible. It was a sight she'd often witnessed, yet it never failed to give her that thrill of mingled fear and excitement.

Shark or dolphin? There was no way of telling.

She tucked her slim, smooth body into the swell of the wave with a deft kick of her flippers, and let the surge carry her effortlessly towards the lonely shore. She had no real expectation that the fish would trouble her. In her experience, all of nature was benign unless proved otherwise, even sharks. And, as the wave broke into a creamy froth all around her, there was no sign of her companion-enemy in the clean, salty water.

Rio was still thinking of that sleek shape as she tugged off her flippers and mask in the shallows, and waded to the beach, bleached hair streaming wetly almost to the uptilted peaks of her breasts. She was naked but for the string of coral round her neck. The small, delicate fragments glinted pink and cream and golden against her deeply-tanned skin.

She did not even consider her nakedness; over the past weeks it had become as natural to her as the ceaseless rumble of the surf, or the impossibly beautiful blue of the vast Australian sky overhead. Besides, the cottage was a hundred and fifty miles from the next human settlement, and more than three hundred miles from Cooktown, the nearest town of any size on the whole coast.

The sun beat down on her flawless skin as she walked to the rock where she'd left her notebooks. She dropped her flippers and mask on the towel, and sat cross-legged beside them to fill in the day's entries. The coral bed out there, beyond the white lines of surf, contained more species than

5

she could ever have imagined.

As she sat, filling in the figures and measurements, Rio Faber seemed as utterly in harmony with the scene as the seagulls that mewed overhead, or the clumps of cocos-palms that arched from the edge of the beach over the turquoise shallows. The flowing lines of her woman's body seemed to have been wind-sculpted, sea-sculpted. Weeks of daily swimming in the often powerful surf had carved away any excess fat, tautening the long, elegant muscles of legs and waist, lifting her breasts and flattening her stomach; just as weeks of nakedness in the East Australian sun had turned her naturally fair skin the rich toffee colour of new bronze, and had bleached the long, thick mop of her golden hair almost platinum-white.

It was only her eyes that seemed at variance with the colours of the Coral Sea. They were the cool, thoughtful grey of a Northern ocean, as if they alone always remembered the misty lands of her birth.

She filled the last line in, then scooped up all her belongings, and trudged up the beach towards the cottage. Once upon a time the sand would have scorched her bare soles unbearably, but now she minded that as little as did the gulls who swooped down to where she'd been sitting, in the vain hope that she'd left them any tidbits.

The cottage itself was sheltered from the sea by a screen of palms, and only a glimpse of its red roof, and the tall, whippy radio aerial rising high above the fronds, betrayed its presence at all. *Her* cottage. She had grown to love it with a fierce, possessive love that rose from deep inside her, and which took no account of the fact that it belonged to the Cotton Foundation.

In fact, the little cottage had been built by Jesse Cotton himself, the Yorkshire-born amateur naturalist whose love for Australia had led him to leave a vast fortune to research directed at 'exploring and preserving the unique Australian heritage, as well as increasing public awareness of its richness'.

Rio did not like to think of the fact that she was only a

guest here. That others had been here before, that when her research was over—in a very few weeks—others would be here when she was back in England. She preferred to think of it as *her* cottage, her home. It was as much a home, after all, as any place she had ever stayed in during her twenty-two years of life.

As she got to the top of the beach, she looked up suddenly, and felt her heart freeze in shock.

A tall man was standing above her, on the path that led to the cottage, staring at her with a mixture of surprise and amusement on his dark face.

She clutched her towel instinctively to cover her nakedness, anger glittering brightly in her grey eyes.

'Who the hell are you?' she demanded fiercely.

'I'm sorry if I startled you,' he said, deep-voiced. His accent, like hers, was English; and he was even more deeply tanned. His thick, curly black hair explained why his skin had transcended her own golden-brown colour to reach a rich mahogany, emphasised by the snowy T-shirt and faded jeans. 'I'm your next-door neighbour, give or take a hundred miles. I've just driven down from Barramundi to see you. I thought you might be on the beach, but I didn't expect you to be . . .' the amusement was more in his eyes than in any smile that crossed his mouth '. . . *au naturel.*'

She stood stiffly, unable to find a word to express her outrage at this intrusion. Her heart was still thudding urgently against her ribs. She knew exactly who he was, now, this powerfully muscled man who towered over her so dominantly. They'd told her about him—somebody Frazer, working a hundred miles up the coast from her, at the house called Barramundi.

'Sharks,' she said grimly, as her mind kicked up the details. The apparently inconsequential word brought a brief smile to his lips.

'That's right,' he agreed. 'I'm the shark man. Cameron Frazer.'

'You'll excuse me if I don't shake hands,' Rio said tersely. her diaphragm had tightened so sharply with the shock of seeing him that she was slightly breathless now, as though she'd been running hard and fast. 'I'd like to get showered and dressed, if you don't mind.'

'Of course.' With grave courtesy, he stepped down to her level, and reached for the belongings she was awkwardly clutching. 'I'll take those for you. Shall we go up to the house?'

Unwillingly, Rio let him take the flippers, goggles and notebooks from her. He was tall enough to make it easy for her to avoid meeting his eyes, but she could see that his naked arms were hard with muscle. The deep V of his T-shirt revealed a sinewy chest and powerful throat, glinting with curling hair. She walked with him up the path, which had been stepped with palm trunks, keeping her towel tightly wrapped around her naked body. That he was here at all was bad enough. That he'd calmly stood there, watching her wander naked up the beach, was intolerable.

'It would have been thoughtful to radio that you were coming,' she rebuked him coldly.

'I tried to contact you,' he said calmly. 'Yesterday and the whole of last night. In fact, your radio silence was the main reason I drove over this morning. Something might have happened to you.' His voice was very deep, matching his height and stature, yet it had a velvety, caressing note that somehow set all her nerves on edge. It grew even silkier as he enquired, 'Is your radio out of action?'

'I forgot to switch it on,' she said shortly, trying not to show any guilt. There were set times when the short-wave radio was meant to be set to 'receive'—especially between eight and ten each night—but she'd got out of the habit weeks ago, preferring the long-drawn sigh of the evening surf to any human voice or news. She saw all the humans she wanted to see during her once-weekly shopping trips to Burgess Cove. 'And nothing's happened to me.'

'I'm glad to hear it.'

She glanced at him with cold grey eyes. She'd been more than faintly prejudiced against Cameron Frazer from the first moment she'd heard his name, thousands of miles away, in London; and his physical presence seemed like an embodiment of all her prejudices.

Another woman would have called him devastatingly handsome. He was obviously over thirty, yet not a single grey strand marked the glossy black richness of his hair, which was over-long, and tumbled almost to touch his broad, formidably muscled shoulders. The raven blackness of those curls, together with his profound tan, gave already vivid blue eyes a stare of stomach-twisting intensity. She had no doubt that if that amiable expression were to turn hostile, Cameron Frazer would possess a quality of male aggression to turn aside all but a crazy few.

A broad face, the jawline and cheekbones hard and uncompromisingly male. Yet the mouth held humour, passionate sensuality, as well as authority. The sort of man who would find nine women out of ten a push-over.

Suddenly more aware than a moment ago of her skimpily covered nakedness, Rio looked away from him. The open-topped red jeep parked beside the cottage explained how he'd got here this morning. The terrible coast roads meant average speeds of less than thirty miles an hour, so it had taken him at least three hours to drive the hundred miles from Barramundi.

'There's some beer in the cupboard if you want it,' she said at the foot of the steps. 'It's warm, though. The fridge broke down last week.'

'Warm beer in this weather?' His smile warmed those deep blue eyes to an almost violet intensity. 'That sounds pretty desperate.'

'I don't touch the stuff,' she said flatly, and turned to walk down the little veranda. 'I'm going to shower now.'

She felt his eyes on her naked back as she padded through the screen door and into her minuscule bathroom. The glittering bubble of her privacy had been well and truly pierced. Damn him!

The water from the big corrugated-iron tank was sun-warmed, but at least it was fresh and sweet. Rio rinsed the

salt from her body and hair, eyes squeezed shut against the
tepid flow.

Cameron Frazer. Her neighbour. She'd never bothered
to make the slightest contact in the six weeks she'd been at
the cottage. Like her, he was doing marine research on this
section of the north-east coast. But they'd made it clear that
Frazer's was *real* research. Sharks, and what made them
occasionally attack humans. Lurid, aggressive, dangerous,
publicity-catching stuff.

Work on corals—prettily coloured, passive things, which
seemed to most lay-people hardly to be living creatures at
all—could scarcely expect to excite the interest, or the
funding, that Cameron Frazer commanded.

Otherwise he wouldn't be living at Barramundi. The old
place had an almost legendary mystique. It was a part of
the history of the Coral Sea, a colonial-style mansion that
had been built by the Prior-Jordan family to supervise
dreamed-of estates, fields of waving sugar-cane which had
long since been swallowed up by the bush. Though the
Prior-Jordans' dream of vast wealth from a sugar empire
had long since died, the great house still stood, dominating
the sweep of Laura Bay.

And it was at Barramundi, named after the fabulous
North Australian game-fish sacred to the Aborigines, that
Frazer had been working for almost three months now.

How, and from whom, he had wangled that particular
site was a mystery to Rio. Whoever was funding him was
evidently a very wealthy patron, for as William Murdoch,
one of the Grant Committee members, had told her in
London, 'He has as fabulous set-up there. He's built great
big salt-water pools, connected by passages to the sea, so
that he can study his objects close-up. All the most
advanced electronic gear, of course, and simply tons of
equipment. But then, of course, his work is of primary
importance.'

'Of course,' she'd echoed drily.

Professor Murdoch had looked solemn. 'You must make
sure you get in touch with him, Miss Faber. Your research

is on a very different level from his, and he has no real
connection with our Foundation, but there's a great deal
you could learn from a man of Frazer's brilliance . . .'

Rio stepped, dripping, on to the cork mat and towelled
herself dry with rather more vigour than was necessary. Of
primary importance, indeed! She hunted among the piles of
shells on the shelf for her hair brush. As she brushed her
long, white-golden hair, she stared at her own face in the
mirror. A young, unlined face that managed to combine
beauty with originality. It didn't need make-up, even if
she'd possessed any, even if she'd wanted to wear any. The
harmony of large, long-lashed eyes and a perfectly shaped
mouth were their own ornament. Fine cheekbones and a
delicate nose ensured that Rio's beauty would only deepen
with the years, and outlast the ravages of time.

She rubbed a spot of cream into her cheeks and forehead,
and touched her full, petal-soft mouth with the little stick of
sunscreen, her mind turning.

How to send Mr Frazer on his way as soon as was
consonant with politeness? She distrusted his motives,
anyway. Men couldn't bear the notion of a pretty woman
living alone in a remote place. Curiosity—and that
predatory male instinct—would have been the real
promptings of this visit, rather than philanthropic concern
about her welfare. The same motives that made the leering
men at Burgess Cove offer their help 'any time you need it,
sweetheart'.

Rio sighed. He *had* driven a hundred miles this morning,
and he *was* a colleague of sorts.

With a flicker of irritation she realised she would have to
offer him lunch, and some attempt at hospitality, including
conversation.

Her bedroom was even more filled with shells and plants
than the bathroom, but it was scrupulously clean and neat.
She pulled on panties and a light blue cotton dress, her
figure needing no other support. The tanned body which
had been so exquisite in its nakedness looked merely slim
and neat in the unfussy clothing. She slipped on sandals,

and clipped the Cartier watch round her right wrist. Against the tanned skin, the gold links and the tiny diamonds glittered with bright opulence.

Another quick glance in the mirror. Don't be too hostile, she told herself briskly, looking into her own cool eyes. He's only a man. She thought again of that dark shape in the wave this morning, vaguely threatening, the dorsal fin stark against the translucent wave. Shark. She was sure of it now. An omen.

When she walked through to find her visitor, he was in the kitchen. He had hauled the gas-powered fridge away from the wall, and had stripped off the back panel. With a flicker of irritation, she noted the neat pile of parts he'd already removed, the jeep's tool kit beside him, his general air of competence. This was exactly the kind of help she could do without.

'Please don't bother trying to fix it,' she said ungratefully. 'I manage perfectly well without it.'

'The motor's jammed,' he replied. 'It won't take a minute to get it going again.'

'It's probably beyond repair,' Rio protested. 'And I don't really need it, anyway——'

Those extraordinarily deep blue eyes silenced her with a glance. 'You can't manage without a refrigerator in this weather,' he said firmly. 'Though I'd have expected the Cotton Foundation to put in something better than this old crock. Any danger of a cup of coffee while I put it all together again?'

Silently, she filled the percolator and set it on the stove, then stood indecisively, watching him work. Every clink and rattle seemed to jar on her nerves; his intrusive male presence in her ultra-private retreat was becoming increasingly annoying, despite the fact that it would be marvellous to have the refrigerator working again. *If* he could fix it.

Beneath the thin T-shirt, the powerful muscles of his shoulders and back moved in clear definition. The denim of his jeans hugged potent thighs and lean hips, emphasising his maleness. Rio considered herself very fit, but this man carried an aura of power and competence that somehow pointed up her own weaknesses.

'You enjoy solitude, don't you?' He didn't look up from his work as he asked the question.

A momentary frown ruffled the smoothness of her forehead. 'I don't mind it,' she replied uneasily.

'No?' He lifted the motor back into the fridge, and started bolting it in with deft fingers. 'But you mind my being here?' That question—or was it a statement?—silenced her for a moment, then she got up to find cups and saucers.

'Not at all,' she replied unconvincingly. 'How are your sharks, Mr Frazer?'

'Thriving. How are your corals, Miss Faber?'

'Surviving.'

'I'm glad to hear it.' He pushed the fridge effortlessly back into place, and turned it on. The familiar purr of the motor indicated a rapid return to normality. 'There,' he said calmly. 'Now you'll be able to have cold beer for your guests.'

'I get very few guests.' Rio tried to sound gracious. 'But thanks all the same.'

'My pleasure.' He washed his hands, then leaned against the bench, studying her with unsettling frankness. 'Look, I'm sorry I happened to see you on the beach just now. It wasn't my intention to spy.' The dark blue gaze drifted over the contours of her dress with that hint of an inner smile. 'If it's any consolation, you have a great deal to be proud of—and nothing at all to be ashamed of.'

Rio felt the heat touch her cheeks. 'Nudity is perfectly natural, Mr Frazer. Shall we say no more about it?'

He nodded. 'Only if you agree to drop the "Mr Frazer" routine. My name is Cameron.'

'My name is Rio.' She turned away from him, grateful for the bubbling percolator that gave her an excuse to avoid his eyes.

'Rio,' he repeated, his deep voice caressing the word.

'Whose idea was it to call you Rio?'

She gritted her teeth, not for the first time in her life regretting that her Christian name was a bizarre one. 'My parents christened me Royale,' she said stiffly. 'My friends called me Rio at school. I prefer it.' He laughed softly, and she arched a slender eyebrow at him. 'Is that funny?' she enquired coolly.

'Not at all.' He accepted the cup she passed him. 'Royale is a beautiful name. A lot of women might have chosen to keep it.'

'It's pretentious and unwieldy.'

'On the contrary, it's musical and feminine. Your parents had excellent taste.' He drank the coffee, black and sugarless, and smiled at her wickedly. 'However, Rio suits you in another way. I shall always think of you naked and natural, in the sea, as Royale. With your skirt on, under a roof, you'll be Rio.'

Now she was blushing fully, the tan in her cheeks unable to disguise the flush of blood. He set the empty cup down, and let his gaze wander through the open doorway into the main room of the cottage. 'Would you mind if I looked around?' he enquired gently.

'Go ahead.' Damning his bright blue eyes, Rio followed helplessly as he walked through. The living-room was filled with the treasures she'd found over her weeks on this unnamed stretch of wilderness. Shells of all sizes and shapes; branches of crimson and white coral; driftwood, starfish, coconut shells, a few bottles that had drifted from God-knew-what distances to land on her beach.

'Extraordinary,' he murmured, almost to himself, his eyes following the arrangement of objects.

Why did he have to make his intrusion so damned thorough? 'Just a lot of rubbish I picked up,' she said dismissively, willing him to get back in his red jeep now, and drive back to Barramundi.

'Oh, no.' He walked over to the mantel, moving with the grace of a stalking animal. 'Not rubbish. You have an eye for beauty, Rio Faber.'

Somehow the fact that he'd understood her motley collection annoyed her far more than if he'd laughed at her and mocked her for gathering it. She said nothing as he moved to her desk, and studied her latest notes, her little library of reference books, the clutter of coral pieces that were labelled and indexed on the rack. 'Is that why you've chosen to study corals?' he asked gently, picking up a rounded lump of brain coral. 'Because their beauty calls to you?'

'I find that question slightly odd.' With the care of someone who has lived alone for a long time, Rio clothed her anger in biting words. 'Coelenterates may not have the obvious fascination of man-eating sharks, but they have other qualities apart from beauty, Mr Frazer. As a marine biologist, it may not have escaped your attention that they have developed a barrier reef which stretches for well over a thousand miles along this coastline.'

'The presence of the Great Barrier Reef has not escaped my attention, no,' he said solemnly. 'I didn't mean to insult you—or your coelenterates.' He replaced the brain coral, and drifted across to the window, looking tall and broad-shouldered against the brilliant sunlight. 'You've been here around six weeks now, haven't you?'

'A month and a half,' she nodded. It seemed like an eternity.

'I've been so damned wrapped up in my work,' he said softly. He leaned against the sill, the muscles of his arms tightening to take his weight, and studied Rio with brooding eyes. 'I meant to keep an eye on you, but somehow the time just slipped by . . .'

'I've been managing perfectly well,' Rio said crisply, stung by the implication. 'I haven't encountered the slightest problem so far.' She ran her fingers through her long hair; in the midday heat it was already drying. His eyes followed the movement of her hands, dwelling on the dazzle of gold that was bright enough to reflect a glow on the white ceiling.

'Where do you buy provisions?' he asked. 'Burgess Cove?'

'I go there once a week, usually.'

'Does the isolation ever frighten you?'

'Isolation from other humans, you mean?' She tilted her eyebrow at him. 'As you remarked just now, I'm not the sociable type. Besides, there's nothing here to harm me. Danger tends to reside in the human factor, don't you agree?'

'People are rather more dangerous than coelenterates, I agree.' He smiled, curved lines bracketing his mouth. 'But it's also a human feature to seek our own kind.'

'Not all humans show that feature,' she retorted. 'You know my work's funded by the Cotton Foundation, don't you? Well, Jesse Cotton didn't need other humans. He lived alone and died alone.'

'Bless his Cotton socks.'

'That's flippant!'

'You make it sound like a crime,' he said gently. 'It's permitted to be flippant now and then.' He studied her for a moment. 'This isn't a hospitable landscape, especially not for single Englishwomen. Your confidence suggests that this isn't your first visit.'

'I went to school in South Queensland,' she told him briefly.

'Name, rank and number,' he murmured. 'You don't give away much, Rio.'

The glance she gave him wasn't friendly. 'Maybe there isn't much to give away.'

There was something, a stormy glitter in those deep blue depths, that revealed he wasn't used to being spoken to like this. Not by young women, anyway. But he simply shrugged his broad shoulders. 'OK. All I seem to be doing is treading on your toes. If you can stretch to a spot of lunch, I'll be on my way.'

'Right.' Relief flooded her heart. With the first real alacrity she'd shown since she'd waded out of the sea that morning, Rio went into the kitchen, and squatted in front of the cupboard.

It was, she realised suddenly, disastrously bare. When the fridge had broken down she'd had to throw away a lot of the fresh food she'd bought last time at Burgess, and she hadn't been shopping in a long time.

'There's a can of mushroom soup,' she called eventually, 'and a packet of crackers. And some noodles. And some eggs.'

'Is that what you were going to have for your dinner?' he asked drily, leaning against the kitchen door. 'Mushroom soup and boiled eggs?'

'I'm very short of food,' she said defensively, knowing he'd be thinking her hopelessly incompetent. 'When the fridge packed in . . .' She glanced up at him. 'I was going to Burgess tomorrow, to restock.'

He grunted, looking as though he were trying not to smile. 'Scrap the lunch, then. I don't want to eat your last noodle. I'll just get back to Barramundi straight away.'

'No!' Suddenly ashamed of her churlishness and her skeletal hospitality, Rio found herself pleading with him. 'Do have something—you can't drive all the way back with nothing in your stomach except a cup of coffee.' She tried a tiny smile. 'A bowl of soup, at least. Please?'

His mouth quirked mockingly. 'Go on, then.'

'Good.' She busied herself with the threadbare meal, wondering what law of the universe decreed that your cupboard had to be at its emptiest when visitors came. Her bowl of soup and noodles wasn't going to go a long way towards sustaining a man of Frazer's size . . .

'Tom Walkinshaw in London told me what your research was about,' he said, watching her prepare the food. 'But I'm afraid I've forgotten the exact details.'

'I'm studying the enemies of corals,' she replied, stirring the soup, 'rather than the corals themselves.'

'Like the crown-of-thorns starfish?' he queried.

'They happen to be the most dramatically obvious predators,' Rio nodded. 'They're horrible things. But it isn't as simple as that. Their attacks are intermittent, and in any case, they've probably been coexisting with corals for billions of years before man took any notice of them. It's man himself who's the greatest destroyer of the coral reefs.'

'Why aren't you in London or Sydney, then,' he smiled, 'studying the enemies of corals in person?'

'I'm trying to assess whether the reef is going to survive mankind at all,' she replied, not answering his smile. 'The Pacific is industrialising at a steady rate. That means that the waters are showing higher and higher levels of silt, industrial chemicals, pesticides and fertilisers from new farming methods, oil, factory effluents—and whatever else is dumped into the sea. You name it.' She shot him a cool grey glance. 'Just about all of it is capable of killing the coelenterates that form corals. Or if it doesn't kill them, it kills the food that they live on, or it encourages the predators that destroy them.'

'And how exactly are you checking on the reef?' he asked.

'I dive, most days.'

His eyes narrowed for a moment. 'You dive every day, alone?' He jerked a thumb in the direction of the surf that could be heard rumbling beyond the palms. 'In that?'

'Unless it's very rough. Why not?' she challenged. 'Surely you have to do a fair bit of diving yourself?'

'Yes, but——' He didn't finish the sentence, and Rio smiled with a hint of sourness.

'I'm a very powerful swimmer, Mr Frazer. As powerful as most men. With flippers, I can manage most surf without trouble. And I'm very careful.'

'You do realise,' he said after a short pause, 'that there are sharks in this water?'

'I've never seen a shark yet,' she shrugged, conveniently dismissing the dark shape in the wave. 'Please don't be concerned about me. I swim out to the reef, take my measurements, and catch the next wave back again. I'm in the water for a maximum of half an hour at a time.'

'Does your Committee happen to approve of the fact that

you're in the habit of going out in the surf daily?' he asked silkily.

'It's my life, Mr Frazer.' Of course the Committee didn't approve. They'd have a communal coronary in their dusty London office if they ever knew how far out she really went! Cameron stared at her with intense blue eyes for a few seconds, until she began to feel quite uncomfortable, then appeared to dismiss the topic.

'And?' he prompted. 'Are the coral reefs going to survive?'

'My study is only a tiny little piece in a very big mosaic,' she said. 'And my grant only covers two months' research. It takes years for a coral colony to grow a few feet. All I can do is log a few measurements, make a few tentative conclusions, and go home.'

'That's an unusually modest assessment,' he said solemnly. 'Most researchers take themselves a lot more seriously.'

'I didn't say that I don't take myself seriously,' she reminded him. Tired of talking about herself, she changed the subject round. 'They told me something about your research, too.' She poured the soup into bowls, and set them out on the pine table. 'Shark attacks, isn't that right?'

'Various kinds of agggressive behaviour in sharks,' he nodded. He tried a spoonful of the soup, then murmured, 'Hmmm, very good,' non-committally.

Rio picked up her own spoon and tackled the horrible stuff doggedly. Despite Cameron Frazer's slightly savage appearance, there was something about him which suggested that his palate was not unaccustomed to the most sophisticated French cuisine.

Which was about as remote from what she'd just made as the moon was from Barramundi. Mentally, though, she dared him to complain about the soup. He hadn't been invited, had he? And the truly annoying thing was that, given the right ingredients, she could have made him a meal that wouldn't have shamed a cordon bleu chef.

The silence that descended was heavy, and unbroken by any conversation. It was an embarrassingly bad meal, and her own discomfort at having to serve it to him was putting her in a thoroughly jaded mood. As if to add insult, there was plenty of soup left in his bowl when he put his spoon down with an air of finality.

'Not hungry?' she asked acidly.

'It's rather hot for mushroom soup,' he smiled. 'Tasty though it was.'

'Don't be so damned tactful!' she rejoined, dropping her own spoon with a plop. 'It's foul. You've just come at a bad time, that's all.'

'Yes,' he said drily, 'that much is patently obvious. Want any help with the washing up?'

'No,' she said shortly, not making any effort to be sociable now.

'Very well,' he said easily. 'Before I go—is there anything else you'd like done around the place?'

Rio struggled with her pride. The flame on the stove had been dwindling rapidly the past few times she'd used it. It was time to change the bottle, but it was a job she hated because of the overpowering weight of the cylinders. 'The gas bottle,' she said at last. 'It's so heavy . . .'

'You want it changed?' He nodded, and walked outside. Rio cleared the table and washed the things while he manhandled the five-foot-high bottle of gas into position against the outside wall of the kitchen. He would be gone, soon, and she would be left to her blissful solitude again.

Solitude. It occurred to her, as she dried the cheap china bowls, that the silence might rush in with rather a heavy note when that red jeep receded into the distance. Unwelcome though his presence had been, it had also been vividly stimulating.

Yeah, she told herself, like sitting on a nettle patch! After weeks alone, any company might seem to have its attractions, even Frazer's.

'All done.' He stood at the kitchen door, utterly unfazed by a job which left her dripping with sweat and limp-armed. 'Is the Land Rover going all right?'

'No problems.'

He didn't waste time on ceremonies, just nodded. 'I'll get along now, Rio.'

'Thanks for dropping by.' *Dropping by* seemed an absurd way to describe a two-hundred-mile round trip, but you got used to talking that way in the Top End. She walked to the jeep with him, taking a final covert look at her uninvited guest.

He was very tall, topping her own golden head by at least a foot. With an athlete's taut waist and wide shoulders, he had a classically masculine figure. Proud of it, too, she thought drily, watching the grace with which he carried himself. A beautiful male animal, equipped with a razor-sharp mind. An achiever.

He swung himself into the open-topped jeep, and looped the safety-belt across his broad chest.

'I don't want to nag you,' he said casually, 'but don't forget to leave your receiver on at night. It's vital for people to be able to reach you.' The dark blue eyes met hers with a directness that suddenly twisted her heart-strings. 'Solitude is both an enemy and a friend, Rio. I've left my number next to your radio. If you need help of any kind, or just to hear a voice, call me up. Understand?'

'Yes,' she said in a small voice, quelled by the tone of his voice. For all his friendliness, there was an authority in his personality that enabled him to make the gentlest hint a command. 'I—I'm sorry about the horrible soup. And thanks for fixing the fridge. It'll be very handy.'

'Naturally.' He smiled into her eyes, as brutally handsome as a tiger. 'Now you can go and put your heart back in it.'

Dumbfounded, she could only stare at him.

His laugh was soft, deep in his throat. 'It's been a most stimulating visit, anyway. Take care in that surf, Rio. Never go out if you have the slightest doubt about anything.'

'I never do,' she promised.

'And never go into the water if you're bleeding, no

matter how slightly. Not ever. Not even ankle-deep. You understand?'

'Yes.'

He held out his hand, and she took it without thinking. He lifted it to his lips, and kissed the back of her hand with warm lips. 'You're very beautiful, Rio,' he said gently.

The engine roared into life as he twisted the key, and with a quick wave he swung the jeep in a wide circle, and accelerated away from the cottage, down the palm-lined road and out of sight.

Rio stood quite still where he'd left her, until the noise of the engine had faded into the dim murmur of the surf, and the dust hung in the hot air, barely moving.

Then she turned, and walked slowly back to the cottage. It seemed to have shrunk. In the corner of the kitchen, the fridge hummed contentedly.

Absently, she opened the fridge door. The internal light shone brightly on the empty glass shelves, the bare racks.

Loneliness overwhelmed her suddenly, bringing the sharp tears prickling to her grey eyes. Damn him! She'd been flawlessly happy in her solitude two hours ago, sitting on the beach, totally at one with the world. Now she was wounded. Now there was a gaping hole somewhere between the vast sea and the vast land and the vast, empty, blue sky.

Now it would take her days to reform that pearl of peace within her shell.

CHAPTER TWO

Rio spent most of the next few days regretting her behaviour. Remembering and regretting.

Cruising out past the breakers, poring over her notes in the baking heat of the cottage, or lying dreamily under the palm trees, Rio found herself rehearsing the abortive

conversation she'd had with Cameron Frazer. And
realising just how prickly she'd been. So many words that
could have been changed, put another way to sound
friendlier, less smart-alecky.

Solitude, he'd said, can be an enemy. That was not a new
lesson for Rio Faber, but one which she'd forgotten, all the
same. In these past six weeks, she'd become very solitary
indeed. A solitary, tawny bobcat, snarling from her lair at
any passer-by.

It filled her with a strange, restless shame to visualise how
he must have seen her—a hostile creature who wandered
around naked, who lived in a shambles of broken shells and
driftwood, with her radio off and her fridge broken. In the
light of that vision, her clever-dick retorts to his enquiries
now made her squirm with embarrassment.

No wonder there had been mockery in that dazzling
smile.

Yet he'd *understood*. Of course he had. Barramundi wasn't
much less isolated than her own cottage. He would
experience loneliness, just as she did. He had been alone
longer, too.

It wasn't that she felt any increasing warmth towards the
man at all, though she did realise how grateful she should
be to him; but his visit had re-awakened her self-
consciousness, and had pricked the balloon of her
complacency.

Rio Faber had been alone for a long time. Nearly half
her life. Not shut away from people, or deprived of
companionship—but alone, all the same. It had started
with the car crash.

She'd been twelve years old when they'd died, the two
people who now lay in a London cemetery, beneath the
single tombstone that read simply, *Paul Faber, Vivienne
Faber*.

She'd adored her parents, with an only child's unques-
tioning love. Their death had been bewildering and
terrible, a blow given added force by the lack of any close
relative to give support and comfort.

Except Maudie. Rio had written a letter of sheer desperation to her father's cousin, from the house in Highgate where she'd been put in care after the accident. The family who'd volunteered to foster Rio had understood almost nothing about her. Their carefully measured kindness had been a daily torment, their apathy towards her surging intellect had been an agonising frustration.

They were friendly, concerned people, but nothing in their experience had prepared them for Rio's exceptional intelligence. They were simply unable to give the soaring wings of her imagination enough air space.

Maudie, reading the fierce, incoherent letter in the sunshine of her Brisbane garden, had understood all. She'd flown to London, an unlikely St George in a grey bun and a floral dress that was far too thin for a London autumn.

As an elderly spinster, Maudie Faber had been totally frank about her capacity to look after a twelve-year-old child.

'It means boarding-school during term-time,' she'd said flatly. 'Durrabundi, where I went. Royale will get a damned good education there, one tailor-made for her. Durrabundi's the only school I know where they really understand that biology means more than book-keeping.'

The social workers who'd come to the house for the meeting had stared in silence at Rio's racks of coral fragments, each branch and crumb catalogued, named, described.

'She needs space,' Maudie had said implacably. 'She needs sun. Look at the kid! Look at those books! Does the average twelve-year-old spend all her pocket-money on books like that?'

One of the social workers had turned his head on one side to read the spines, and had found himself unable to pronounce most of the words in the titles.

So they'd packed her clothes and her books, and her 'collection of sticks and stuff', and Royale Faber had gone to live in Australia for the next six years.

Maudie had become her second mother, during school

holidays, at any rate. It had been a relationship that Rio looked back on with great affection, acknowledging a debt of gratitude that she could never now repay. It had been Maudie who'd really made her a biologist, not school or university.

Rio switched on the transistor radio as the sun sank crimson into the dim blue hills, staining the sea to the distant horizon. Absently, she listened to the news, and the cheerful Australian voices on the airwaves.

'Entertainment for Top End listeners, provided by your favourite and mine, Slim Dusty, singing a selection of great ballads . . .'

She lay back on the veranda, and let the easy music wash over her. 'Is that why you've chosen to study corals? Because their beauty calls to you?' Yes. That had been the start of it, though she'd given him an elusive answer. The exotic quality of corals had drawn her since babyhood. She'd dreamed of them. Their vivid colours and fairyland shapes had taken her developing mind to distant strands and golden places, beneath blue seas and violet skies, to where the thunder of surf and the sound of the tropical wind through palm fronds sang loud in her ears, drowning out the sound of London traffic and the greyness of London rain.

The earthly paradise of her imagination hadn't been as specific a place as Australia, not until she'd gone to live there, joyfully released from bondage by Maudie. But in Australia, Rio had found that elusive paradise of the imagination.

And the reality of Australia had taught her that corals weren't just pretty fragments of coloured bone. At Durrabundi she'd learned that the tiny creatures which formed corals had raised the greatest structure ever laid on the face of the earth by living beings. A chain of reefs over a thousand miles long, easily visible from the moon, creating an immense lagoon that had for ever changed the coastline of North-Eastern Australia.

Years later, taking her degree in marine biology at

Oxford, that initial wonder had remained undimmed.

It was during her final exams that Rio had been orphaned a second time. The diabetes which Maudie had for so long kept in abeyance had finally called in its long-standing debt. And Rio's grief had found a tangible outlet—to fulfil the keen hope that Maudie had always had in her talent.

From Oxford, she'd contacted the Jesse Cotton Foundation, the prestigious organisation which offered Rio her best chance of getting funds to research in Australia. It was one of the few scientific foundations not over-burdened by applicants with obscure and selfish briefs. Work funded by Cotton had to be significant. It accepted only the cream of researchers, and favoured those whose work would enhance the harmony between man and nature.

Their award of a grant, after a three-hour interview with Rio, had been as big a boost to her as getting her first-class degree.

It was an entrée into the kind of career she really wanted—working to preserve the sunlit word she loved so much. Once she'd finished her work here, her chances of getting a job with a prestigious employer, like Clyde Laboratories, or Biotechnology Systems, were far higher.

Merton had put a polish on her, as it did to all its daughters. But the pattern of her life had cast Rio in a different mould from the other girls at the famous Oxford college. She'd grown up to be self-sufficient, almost aggressively so. The tender sides of her nature, too, had turned inward, away from potential harm.

She'd had two love affairs at Oxford, but neither had lasted long or ended happily. She'd been far too intelligent not to see that it was only her body that was wanted; and she'd lacked the ability to deceive herself into pretending otherwise.

Men had not been able to fill that aching void inside her; nor had she offered love in return. Most had found her wary gaze far too intelligent for comfort, her mind too cold and slippery to flatter their vanity.

All of which might, had he known it or guessed at it, have given Cameron Frazer some insight into her behaviour on the day he'd met her.

The weather had been growing increasingly muggy for several days, dull grey skies somehow increasing the heat until it seemed that the whole world was wilting.

The humidity drove Rio into the sea eight or ten times a day, to sprawl luxuriously in the cool shallows, peering for shells in the wet sand. Since Cameron's visit, she'd taken to bringing her redundant costume down with her, and keeping a wary eye on the path; but there was no further sign of him.

Nor, she reflected, bobbing in the waves, had he called her up on the short wave, though she'd somehow half expected him to. She herself was too shy, or too diffident, to bother calling him. She'd always left the onus of social contact to others, anyway; besides, she had nothing to announce or complain of.

When she next swam out to the reef, the surf was unexpectedly powerful. As a teenager, she'd learned the knack of sliding underneath the breakers, swimming hard and fast between waves to get herself beyond the cycle of the surf, to where the water was sixty feet deep, and the most luxuriant coral growth began.

The reef was a bewilderingly beautiful place to visit. Though she'd come to know the coral beds as well as any stretch of terra firma, she never failed to find something wonderfully new, some plant or creature totally beyond her knowledge. When she dived, it was like entering another world, a world where colours and shapes had suffered a sea-change. The water was almost always pellucid, the moonscape of the reef haunted with fish of a thousand different hues.

But this time she found herself breathless by the time she'd made it there, her back and arms burning with the intense effort. The undertow was strong, sweeping her sideways in long, tiring movements, forcing her to keep swimming just to stay where she wanted to be.

The water, too, was murky, and there was little pleasure in her dive. She was fully aware that sharks seemed to feed more actively when the water was cloudy and, almost for the first time ever, she felt a sense of relief as she waded tiredly ashore, tossing her flippers and mask on to the towel.

There was an uneasy stillness in the air, a thundery, ominous feeling. The palm fronds hung flaccidly down, and the leaden sky overhead seemed claustrophobically low.

Depression had settled firmly over Rio. She trudged up to the cottage, went on to the veranda, and switched on the radio to get a weather report.

A symphony concert was in progress, Brahms' second. Leaving it on, Rio showered and changed, and was combing her platinum-white hair lazily in the kitchen when the tail-end of the news sent her hurrying back to the radio.

'. . . and at present it looks as though Trixie is going to pass within a hundred kilometres of Darwin between 14.00 hours and 16.00 hours tomorrow. Strong winds and high seas are expected in the area as the cyclone passes westward. There now follows a warning for shipping in the Gulf of Carpentaria.'

Rio listened to the shipping report, her eyes fixed on the grey patch of sea visible through the palms. Cyclone Trixie. Why did cyclones always have to be female? And what mindless meteorological male chose the invariably coy, cute-little-girl names? She went back into the kitchen, and read the Cyclone Action Warning that hung on the wall, next to the fridge.

Her expression was sombre. The dire warnings to ensure a supply of provisions and water, to board up the windows and doors, were not exactly reassuring in the light of her position at the cottage. It had been days since she'd been to Burgess to stock up. The fridge was almost empty, and there was practically nothing in the cupboard now. She cursed her own laziness and stupidity. Instead of mooning over

Cameron Frazer, she should have made extra shopping trips, got herself organised!

'If a cyclone is imminent,' she read, 'you should anchor yourself to a secure fixture, beneath a substantial shelter.

Beside this advice, someone had scribbed 'e.g. crawl under the bed' in pencil, but whether that had been intended as a joke, or as a serious suggestion, Rio was undecided.

It was cyclone weather, that was certain. The barometer in the living-room was almost a toy, but it showed a steadily dropping mercury. And the muggy heat was hateful, making even the slightest of movements an effort. She was barely ten minutes out of her shower, and already her tanned skin was damp with perspiration. She found herself staring up at the roof, wondering exactly what 'a substantial shelter' was.

Cameron radioed her at eight. Through some telepathy. Rio had known in her heart that he would call; but it was so many weeks since she'd last used the complex short-wave set that she'd almost forgotten the instructions Liaison had given her, and for a while she bungled her attempts to answer his signal.

Then she got through. The sound of his deep voice, distorted by electronics though it was, had a decidedly soothing effect on her nerves.

'What's the weather like at your end?' he asked.

'No wind at all.' Her voice was rather higher than normal. 'But it's terribly hot and steamy. And the mercury's dropping all the time.'

'What's it down to now?' he asked.

'There's no reading at all.'

He grunted. 'Ever been in the vicinity of a cylone before?'

'No,' she said.

'It can be unsettling. Read the Action Warning, Rio. There should be one in the kitchen.'

'I've read it,' she said. 'All that stuff about storing water and food—well, I—I've been running a bit low lately.'

His curse drifted clearly out of the static. 'What exactly have you got to eat, then?'

'Not much,' she said in a small voice. 'I was going to go tomorrow——'

'Not tomorrow.' That unquestionable command was in his voice now. 'Listen to me, Rio. Tomorrow is definitely *not* the day to go anywhere. It could be extremely rough. You understand?'

'Yes,' she said, thinking of those compelling blue eyes.

'Tomorrow is going to be a very good day for staying indoors with a thick book. Have you got a pen and paper handy?'

'Yes——'

'Write down this list of things, then do them all as soon as you sign off.'

'I'm ready.' She nodded, pulling the pad over.

'Fill the Land Rover's tank now, and get it under cover. Shutter the windows—I know it's hot, but do it all the same. Don't open them until the danger's past. Fill as many receptacles with water as you can, and get them in a safe place. Get the first-aid kit out of the bathroom, and keep it handy. Get anything precious in as safe a place as you can find. Am I going too fast?'

'I've got all that,' she said uneasily.

'It's unlikely that the cyclone will come anywhere near you,' he went on. 'But if you hear that it's changed direction, or you think it might be coming too close, turn off the gas bottles. Go to the bedroom. Shut the door and bolt it. Get a sheet; and tie yourself to the bed with it.'

'You're joking!' she gasped.

'The bed is bolted to the floor,' he said drily. 'It's about the most solid thing in the cottage. If you can, use the mattress, or at least the blankets, to protect yourself from flying rubbish, and keep the transistor by you all the time, tuned to Radio Darwin. If there's any danger, you'll hear hourly warnings.'

'OK.' She looked at the list of tasks with cloudy grey eyes.

'I don't like the sound of this one little bit,' she confessed.

'You'll be all right,' he said gently. 'Trixie is set to pass you by a long way. But there will certainly be nasty winds. Just use your head. I'll drive through to see you when the weather dies down.'

'There's no need for that,' she said, the cool response reflex-quick.

'Who's talking about *need*?' he retorted. 'I'd like to come. Maybe you'll take me out to your pet reef, and we can dive together?'

Rio struggled to suppress the hostile reaction that had sprung to her lips. She didn't want that kind of intimacy. All she'd wanted was a human contact against the dark backdrop of the imminent bad weather. 'If you like,' she said at last, her voice stiff and unwelcoming.

'You're being unusually docile tonight,' he said, and she could hear the warm smile in his voice. 'I won't come if you don't want me, Rio. But I'll stay in touch on the short wave.'

'Thanks,' she said shortly.

'Now go and get all those jobs done. And do I have to tell you to stay out of the water?'

'No. It was rough today.'

'It'll be rougher tomorrow,' he assured her. 'Anything more?'

She thought hard. 'I don't think so . . .'

'Then I'll sign off. Take care.'

'I'll try.'

'Goodnight, Rio.'

'Wait!'

'What is it?' he asked patiently.

'Will—will you be all right at Barramundi?' she asked, the question almost involuntary.

'Nothing much bothers me,' he said with a soft laugh. 'I'll be busy taking care of my staff. Sweet dreams. Over and out.'

His *staff*? With a snort, Rio realised that his living conditions at Barramundi must be even more luxurious than she'd realised!

It took her two hours to get everything done, and she was weary to the bone by the time she tumbled into bed in the stifflingly hot bedroom.

Despite that, Rio was awake at dawn, as she almost invariably was these days. She peered cautiously through the shutters. The sky was clear, and the glory of the sunrise out of the sea was dazzling.

The air, too, was cool and fresh. She inhaled a deep lungful, grateful that the mugginess had passed at last. By the looks of it, Trixie was not going to bother her today.

Nevertheless, she didn't stray from the cottage all morning, despite the steadily rising temperature, and she kept the transistor radio on, as Cameron had commanded.

By noon, the blue water looked deliciously inviting, and her resistance melted in the heat. She ran down the beach to the water and plunged in, revelling in the cool waves that cleansed her overheated body.

Wearing only shorts and a skimpy top, she spent the afternoon cross-legged in the shade of the palms, writing without haste in her several notebooks.

The day ended as beautifully as it had begun, the few clouds in the clear sky only serving to add beauty to the sunset. Rio relaxed on the veranda, thinking with mild irritation that she could have gone to Burgess Cove today, after all. She was starving by now, and the only things left in the cupboard could not by any stretch of the imagination be called appetising.

Never mind, she would go tomorrow. Oddly, though, the transistor radio was no longer picking up Darwin, though she could get any number of Indonesian stations with ease. Guiltily wondering whether Cameron had tried to contact her while she'd been on the beach, she connected the short wave to its battery of power calls and radioed Barramundi.

But he wasn't answering. She tried several times without result.

Instead, she eventually raised a bored North Queensland farmer.

'Receiving you loud and clear, RX 105. You got a

problem there? Over.'

'Not really,' she replied. 'I was just wondering about Cyclone Trixie.'

'Cyclone Trixie's done a U-turn, girl. Whereabouts are you?'

'On the coast,' she called back. 'Cape York Peninsula, around twelve degrees latitude.'

'Stand by, please.' There was a short pause, and then the boredom went right out of the slow voice. 'Bloody hell! You got someone there with you? Over.'

'I'm on my own,' she said with a sinking heart. 'What's the news? Over.'

'The news is you'd better get your head down, girl. Cyclone Trixie's kicking up a hell of a storm in the Torres Straits right now. And she's heading your way.'

The wind had started rising shortly after nine, by which time she'd stopped trying to raise Cameron, in despair.

Rio had been through tropical storms before, and at first she could even find some enjoyment in the wild rain that lashed at the windows, and the angry rumble of the distant surf.

But this storm was different. It reached no perceptible peak. It just kept on intensifying. By midnight, it had become a savage onslaught that went beyond any-thing she'd ever experienced. The whole cottage was groaning and creaking, the roof starting to rattle as though it were about to physically rise up and fly away. The shutters rattled and slammed like machine-gun fire all around, but they weren't loud enough to drown out the thundering surf that was now clearly higher up the beach.

She sat on the bed, afraid and alone, her hands clenched between her denim-clad knees. It was pitch-dark because she'd shut the gas off hours ago. The torch lay beside her, next to the first-aid kit and the transistor radio. Something crashed outside, then clattered away into the general uproar. The lid of the water-tank, she guessed, flipped off like a bottle-cap. 'God, Cameron,' she whispered, 'where *are* you?' Suddenly, she badly needed the male companionship she'd scorned before. When the world was tearing itself apart, humans ought to be together.

The howling noise was like some vast beast that had the whole house in its jaws. Should she tie herself to the bed, the way Cameron had commanded? Even in the fear of the moment, that seemed an extravagant gesture. The little house, was, after all, holding up, and she was safe in its shelter.

So far.

She rolled herself, fully clothed, in the bedclothes, and shut her eyes, wondering whether she would sleep a wink this night.

Over the next hour, she realised exactly how far she'd underestimated the violence of a cyclone. An immensity of noise exploded around the cottage, as though all that had gone before had been a feeble prelude to the main event. An eruption of demented, elemental rage that signalled the arrival of Trixie.

The cottage swayed drunkenly, mocking its former strength, and Rio screamed, sitting up and clutching for her torch. In its beam, she could see the rafters of the roof twisting jerkily, dust and splinters pouring down at her. In the vast torrent of noise outside, she could clearly hear the first palm trunks splintering and rending. The very floorboards under her feet were surging perceptibly as the wind pumped itself under the house with malevolent and terrifying power.

With shaking hands, Rio looped the sheet around her slim waist, and knotted it tightly to the welded-iron frame of the bed.

Somewhere in the house, a window exploded like a grenade, then another, and then the wind was inside the house. She cowered in terror as her bedroom door burst open, hurling a mass of debris into the room. The door slammed twice against its hinges with savage force, and then the wind ripped it off contemptuously, and flung it across the room like a playing-card.

Trixie was a titanic devil, hurling the contents of the cottage at Rio with murderous violence. A lurid flare of lightning revealed a glimpse of chaos to her staring eyes. The floor was littered with her books and specimens, the precious pages of her notebooks whirling like confetti, the shattered remains of the cheap furniture spread everywhere.

The long, agonised tearing sound outside her window made her scream again. The veranda, she knew, was being crushed and stripped away, and with it the water-tank, and probably the bathroom, too.

She was being showered with rubbish constantly, rivets from the iron roof, bits of wood and chipboard, disjointed fragments of the life she'd led here for seven weeks.

Furniture slammed around in the room next door, like dice in some giant dice-box. More windows were bursting inward now, and something lashed across her shoulders like a flail, knocking the breath out of her body. She clung to the iron bars of the bedhead, her face buried in the pillows, and prayed for life, beyond tears or terror.

Her bedroom window was probably the last one to go. It blew like a cannon shot and, by some freak of atmospheric pressure, most of the debris in the room surged out of the window and into the night.

In exchange, rain tore into her room, stinging like thin chains, drenching her in seconds. There was no escape now. Trixie clawed at her with iron nails, hauling at Rio's slight body, straining at the bonds she'd anchored herself with.

For a few seconds, the onslaught receded. Squinting fearfully through the fair hair that slashed at her face. Rio caught a lightning-flash glimpse of the outside world through the gaping hole where the window had been.

She could hear the sea thundering among the palm grove, uprooting the trees and carving the land. But the sounds of destruction were steadily being drowned out. The noise of the wind was unbelievably vast, a totality of anger that crushed everything else into insignificance.

Rio tightened herself into a ball of self-control, setting her mind to the single task of enduring the tyranny of this great monster.

For the next age, there was no sound but the sound of the wind—until the roof finally started tearing away, bit by bit. The tormented squealing of the iron sheets rose above the explosive roar of the wind. It took a bare few minutes to complete the destruction, the final segments peeling away like the joints of an overcooked chicken, leaving Trixie to tower over the house, reaching down at Rio with those insistent, murderous claws.

The wind had stripped everything off the bed by now. It roared through the shell of the house, snatching up every loose thing remaining, and hurling the wreckage far and wide. After that, Rio lapsed into a kind of stupefied semi-consciousness, clinging to the remnants of her shelter with a blind, animal instinct to survive.

It was still dark when she became conscious that the wind was starting to drop. The first sign was that she could hear the remnants of the roof clanking wildly as they flapped against the rafters. Rio clung to the bed, listening with dazed senses as that terrible bellow slowly became a roar. The extreme conditions were settling down to a merely violent storm. She started to cry a little, so grateful to have survived. She was soaked to the skin, aware now that she was shivering helplessly with the cold.

As the first fitful gleams of light appeared in the sky, the storm dropped with extraordinary suddenness. Silence descended with such abruptness that Rio could hear the receding wind travelling down the coast. It was a silence that was eerily unbroken. No cry of bird or rustle of leaves could be heard, and even the surf was muted, as though the waves themselves were creeping in fear of Trixie's return.

'Oh, God!' Rio sat up stiffly, sniffing, and started tugging at the knot of her sheet with nerveless fingers. 'Oh, God . . .'

Blearily, she rose on unsteady legs, peering round her in the grey light.

Devastation.

Every window and door in the cottage had been broken. Most of the roof was gone, the triangles of the remaining roof-trusses stark against the dawn sky. Chaos reigned in the living-room. Not one stick of furniture, not one object of any sort, remained intact. It was all smashed, strewn, trampled into the floor.

The heavy desk was on its side, most of the drawers tumbling their contents out. All her books—scattered. The typewriter—in two pieces. A few pages of her report lay sodden in odd crevices; where the hundreds of others were, God alone knew.

Rio touched the hard, flat bulge in her waistband. The two most important notebooks were still with her. She ached for the work she'd have to do, re-writing the report, but at least the measurements she'd taken over the past weeks were still intact, saved by some instinct that had made her button them into her tight-fitting jeans.

Picking her way through the debris, she poked her head cautiously out of the gaping doorframe. Devastation and more devastation! The veranda had collapsed like a row of dominoes, as she'd suspected. Its timbers lay scattered for hundreds of yards, along with most of the bathroom.

The palm grove was a piteous sight. All the trunks had lost their fronds; many lay smashed on the ground, and many more tilted at crazy angles. She could clearly see the beach beyond, strewn with rubbish of all kinds. The sea was a muddy grey, and oddly motionless, and she knew that the cyclone would have wrought untold destruction in the coral beds out there. It would be days before she could dive again to determine how much damage had been done. And her research, she thought wryly, might have a very different conclusion from the one she'd first envisaged.

In the meantime, however, she had to get to civilisation.

It was pointless hunting for the short wave, because in any case the tall mast was down, and she had no way of re-erecting it alone. She'd be unable to contact Cameron until she got to a telephone—at Burgess Cove, where she could also get something to eat.

She lowered herself to the wet sand, and went in search of the Land Rover. But the corrugated-iron garage had utterly gone, and with it the big grey long-wheelbase Land Rover that belonged to the Foundation.

Unconsciously, she echoed the Queensland farmer of yesterday evening. 'Bloody hell. Where are you, car?'

The increasing brightness of the sunrise answered her. A little grey box lay several hundred yards down the beach, half in the water. She started towards it, and had got half-way there when, with incredulity, she made out the wheels, and the Cotton Foundation logo on the door. It was on its side, like a discarded toy. The wavelets were licking round the cab. Despite its weight, its high sides had made it easy prey for the wind.

Rio ran her hands through her tangled blonde hair, feeling it gritty with sand. So much for Burgess Cove. Maybe she ought to hunt out the transmitter, after all.

The sky overhead was hazy, weirdly lit. All around her that deathly hush reigned. A dead gull lay broken on the ground in front of her. With a grimace, Rio headed back to the cottage, starting to feel the cuts and bruises all over her body.

She thought it was her imagination when she heard the shout from the cottage. Her ears were still ringing from the roar of the wind. But when she caught a glimpse of something moving up among the wreckage, she broke into a run, her heart thumping painfully against her ribs.

Somebody *was* calling! With disbelief, she saw Cameron Frazier's tall figure emerge from the door of the cottage, and start waving as he caught sight of her.

CHAPTER THREE

Rio threw herself into his arms with a sob, and buried her face against his broad chest. Arms that were potently, wonderfully protective, swung her off the ground, spun her round like a child.

'Rio . . .' In contrast to her tears, Cameron was laughing as he set her down, and unhitched the rucksack he'd been carrying. 'I thought you'd been blown to New Guinea! Are you all right?'

She nodded, still too choked up to speak. He held her at arm's length for a moment, looking her up and down with careful blue eyes. Then he took her pale face in his hands, and kissed her hard on the mouth. His lips were warm, comfortingly possessive, and she responded by clinging to his neck with a passion undreamed-of twenty-four hours ago.

'How did you *get* here?' she demanded, finding her voice shakily.

'In the jeep.' He nodded down the littered track, 'It's a quarter of a mile down there. The road's blocked by palm tree trunks.'

'You *drove*? From Barramundi? In that terrible wind?'

'I took shelter during the worst of it.'

'It blew the Land Rover into the sea!'

'It blew me off the road, too,' he nodded. 'The jeep's not exactly in perfect condition, either.' He dismissed it impatiently. 'I'll tell you about it later. We don't have a lot of time, Rio.'

'What do you mean?' she asked, reaching up to touch the dried blood she'd suddenly noticed on his forehead. He'd taken a battering getting here, and his tanned face reflected her own tiredness.

'I mean that this is only the half-way point,' he said. 'We're in the calm Eye, Rio. Didn't you know that?'

'It didn't occur to me.' She sagged slightly as realisation

39

hit her. 'You mean ... it's going to come back?'

'From a different direction.' He nodded. 'This is the dead centre. And there's no way of telling how long we've got. Where's the short-wave set?'

'I don't know,' she said dully, appalled at the prospect of having to face that immense fury again. 'It was on the veranda. The aerial's down, anyway ... Thank God you're here. I tried to reach you last night——'

'I was already on my way here.' He walked to the wreckage of the veranda, and started hauling the broken timbers away. Boneless with the delayed emotion of seeing him, Rio sank down on to a fallen palm trunk, and watched his powerful figure with dazed eyes. His denims and anorak were soaked and torn, and the thick curls of his black hair were stiff with salt and sand. With a grunt of triumph, he squatted, and tugged the black box out of the tangle. 'The battery's here, too. See if you can find some wire, girl.'

Wearily, Rio rose to her aching legs, and made for the standard lamp she could see lying among the broken furniture. She pulled the flex out of the wall, and dragged the whole thing over to where Cameron was setting up the radio. 'Will this do?'

'I hope so.' He pointed at the rucksack. 'Think you could make a fire of some kind? I've brought some food in that.'

'I'm just about dead with hunger.' She laughed breathlessly.

'So am I.' He smiled up at her briefly. 'We'll try and get a hot meal before Trixie gets back.'

Feeling a great deal more cheerful, Rio started rounding up as much dry wood as she could find. There were matches in the kitchen drawers, which were still intact, and by the time she'd got a blaze going Cameron had looped the wire flex over the top of the remaining rafters, and was calling the coastguard.

She stood in silence for a while, the acrid smoke from the fire curling around her, and listened to his repeated attempts to raise a human voice. 'I couldn't get anyone last night,' she warned him. He didn't reply, and she went to hunt in the kitchen for some usable cooking utensils. A few pots and bits of cutlery were still lying around; more importantly, a few gallons of the water she'd stored were still there, under the skeleton of the kitchen sink.

While she was rummaging for more treasures, though, the coastguard's voice came faintly through the crackling static.

'Receiving you, RX 105. Do you read me? Over.'

'Receiving you with difficulty, coastguard. We've just got a temporary aerial here. Over.'

Rio went over to him as the crackly voice asked, 'You got there without injury?'

'More or less.'

'What's the situation, RX 105?'

'The girl's unharmed,' Cameron replied, glancing at Rio, then up at the weirdly hazy sky. 'We're in the calm Eye right now, waiting for developments. There's still some shelter remaining. Over.'

'You're advised to get to it soon. You've probably got less than an hour and a half,' the coastguard warned, and his voice floated away into a blaze of static for a minute. Cameron sat in tense silence, waiting for reception to improve. When the voice drifted back, all they caught was the tail-end of a question.

'Could you repeat please, coastguard? Over.'

'Do you want to be picked up, RX 105? Over.'

'Yes!' Rio said urgently. But Cameron was already speaking.

'Negative, coastguard. Thanks for the offer, but it just isn't worth it.'

'What are you *saying*?' Rio said fiercely, stepping off the remains of the veranda beside him. 'Of course they should pick us up!'

'We're going to get under shelter in a short while,' Cameron went on, ignoring her completely. 'Will you please try to re-establish contact after the cyclone passes?'

'Will do, RX 105. Please take every precaution. We have

reports of winds up to two hundred and fifty kilometres. Over.'

'That sounds about right,' Cameron said drily.

'Tell them to come and pick us up before the cyclone comes back!' Rio demanded in angry incomprehension. 'They can't just leave us here!'

'Your signal's getting very faint, coastguard.' Cameron twisted the volume knob up to full. 'I'm going to sign off now. We might not be able to transmit again after the cyclone passes, but we should be fine. Please pass that message on to the Jesse Cotton Foundation.' He waited for some acknowledgement, but only the crackle of atmospherics answered. 'Over,' he said quietly. 'And out.'

In a fury, Rio slammed down the aluminium pan she'd salvaged. 'What the hell did you do that for?' she demanded, close to tears. She felt the desperation of a castaway, watching a passing ship dwindle on the horizon. 'How can you be so bloody complacent about our chances of surviving? They could have taken us off——'

'There simply isn't time.' He rose, tall and authoritative, and stared her fierce gaze down. 'Men would be risking their lives pointlessly coming out in a helicopter,' he said in his deep voice. 'And as for a boat—you can see it simply isn't possible.'

Tearfully, she stopped and picked up the pan. 'They might have made it,' she choked.

'And they might have died,' he said quietly. 'I risked my own life getting here, Rio.'

'I know.' She gulped down anger and pain in the same hard swallow, and fought to get back control of her emotions. 'I'm sorry, I really am.' She dipped her fingers in the water she'd been carrying, and reached up to clean the dried blood from his forehead, her eyes still brimming with bright tears. 'We are going to be all right, aren't we?'

He leaned forward to kiss her quivering mouth. 'Yes,' he promised gently, 'we're going to be fine.'

'You're hurt.' Her delicately exploring fingers had found an ugly gash down his temple, and a swelling. 'I don't know where the first-aid kit is, either!'

'No matter now.' He smiled, eyes as deep and warm as the sea. 'Let's get some food into our bellies before Trixie gets back. Do you want to cook it?'

'Yes. I'll do a better job than last time,' she vowed.

'Good.' He passed her the rucksack, and she pulled it open.

The food was wrapped in a tin-foil package. She unfolded it, and stared at the contents. Two massive steaks, a dozen links of sausage, and some thick slices of bread.

'Is this all you've brought?' she asked in a strangled voice.

He glanced at her with a slight smile. 'What did you expect?'

'Not this!' She put the steak down with an expression of horror. 'I'm a vegetarian!'

Cameron leaned back against the wall, powerful shoulders taking his weight. 'A vegetarian,' he repeated flatly, his expression dry.

'Yes!'

'Well, today you're a carnivore,' he said silkily. 'It didn't occur to me that you'd be a vegetarian.'

'It never does,' she snapped, the ache of her hunger tormenting her now.

'I'm sorry that I didn't think to fill the rucksack with cheese salad,' he sighed, picking up the meat. 'But I'm afraid you're going to have to make an exception this time.'

'I can't possibly eat that,' she said bitterly. 'I haven't eaten meat in a year and a half.'

'Well, by the time you get to your next bowl of soya beans,' Cameron pointed out grimly, 'you could be dead. You need the protein, Rio. Now forget your principles for ten minutes, and let's get ourselves fed before the other half of Trixie arrives.'

He didn't understand. People never did. She set her pretty mouth in a tight line as she watched him spear the steaks deftly on a stick, and prop them over the shimmering heat of the flames. She'd joined the vegetarian society at

Oxford in her second year; it had been an easy step for her, especially since Maudie had been a lifelong vegetarian, and had given her a good idea of what decent vegetarian cooking could be like. 'I'm not eating meat for *any* reason,' she said grimly. 'Not now or ever.'

'Where did you shelter overnight?' he asked, ignoring her declaration. 'In the bedroom, like I told you?'

'Yes,' she answered shortly.

He glanced at the cottage. 'The place looks pretty rickety now,' he said thoughtfully. 'I don't know how those walls are going to stand up to any more pressure.'

'So where will we go?' she asked unhappily.

'Under the house,' he said decisively. She followed his blue eyes. The cottage had been built on a brick foundation a yard or so high. At regular intervals, there were openings into the dark void underneath, just wide enough to admit a man.

'Ugh!' she said miserably. She'd always had a horror of that dark space underneath Top End houses, which she associated with lizards, snakes and scorpions.

'It's by far the safest place,' he said, reading her thoughts. 'But it'll be sandy. We'll rig up a shelter under there when we've eaten.'

In a few more minutes the steaks were sizzling fat into the flames, their delicious barbecue aroma torment in Rio's nostrils. She turned away, and stared out across the murky sea.

'Most of my report's on its way to Hawaii by now,' she mourned. 'I kept the important notes safe, but it's going to take weeks to write it all out again.'

'I'm sorry,' he commiserated. 'But you *are* alive. Let's try and keep it that way, Rio.'

She turned to see him offering her a piece of perfectly cooked steak, sandwiched between two slices of bread. The saliva rushed into her mouth with humiliating eagerness, but she shook her head determinedly. 'No'

'Eat it.'

'I won't!'

'You will,' he said grimly.

She clenched her teeth. 'Never.'

Cameron rose fluidly from where he was squatting by the fire and walked over to her. 'I didn't drive a hundred miles through a tropical cyclone to argue with a spoiled child.' His voice was calm, but the mahogany-tanned face was wearing an expression that didn't admit of any compromise. 'If you don't eat it, Rio, I'm going to get straight back in my jeep and leave you here to work things out on your own.'

'*No!*' she said urgently, grey eyes widening in horror.

'Then eat.'

She stared from his implacable blue eyes to the piece of meat. 'You bastard!' she said tightly.

'That's right,' he agreed genially. He put it into her hand, and started to eat his own rough sandwich with calm thoroughness.

It wasn't a situation that allowed any show of pride. Rio looked at the food with cold anger, then started to eat the first meat she'd tasted in eighteen months.

It was delicious, and physically there was no ordeal in getting it down. Mentally, she was filled with revulsion that was compounded of fury against him for forcing her to eat it, and bitterness at her own hungry body that accepted the nourishment with such mindless eagerness.

He finished long before her, and licked his fingers clean, glancing at her with speculative eyes.

'OK?' he asked quietly.

Rio nodded sullenly, chewing at the rich meat with dogged resentment. He kicked the fire out, crushing the embers with the soles of his leather boots, then started shifting things under the house, starting with the short-wave set.

Covertly, she tossed the last piece of the sandwich aside, and moved to help him, wiping her greasy fingers on her jeans.

'They said around an hour and a half,' he grunted, pushing the radio as far along as he could. 'That gives us only a short while more. See if you can find some sheets.'

She obeyed. In the meantime, he hauled the mattress off the bed, and dragged it under the cottage, doubling it up to get it through the entrance-hole. He possessed awesome physical strength, she guessed, coupled with the knowledge and will to use it effectively. His body moved with the smooth grace of an animals, a purposeful, dangerous male animal that knew exactly what he was doing.

And how to get his own way.

The food was warm in her stomach, the strength from it already flowing into her veins, bringing back energy and stamina.

There had been an imperceptible darkening in the eerily lurid sky for the past few minutes, and the way Cameron glanced upwards showed that it had not escaped him, either.

'It's time we made ourselves secure,' he said gently. 'You take the rucksack. Ready?'

'Yes,' she said, slightly breathless. He lowered himself through the square hole, squeezed his wide shoulders through, then held out a brown hand to her.

'Come.'

She took his hand, fighting down her instinctive distaste of going into a dark, confined space, and let him guide her through the opening.

The ground was sandy, but unexpectedly clean, and in the darkness she could just make out the joists and floorboards up above. The crawl-space was barely two feet high. She followed Cameron, imitating his slithering movements, hauling his rucksack after her.

At the darkest point, far underneath the cottage, a brick pier rose up to support the floor. As she arrived, he was tying the first sheet around it.

'This is the most sheltered part of the whole structure,' he said, his eyes glinting in the darkness. 'Pass me the rucksack.'

'What's going to happen to your jeep?' she asked, her voice hollow in the confined area.

'I'm more worried about what's going to happen to us.'
He tied a final knot, and then she felt strong, sandy fingers
closing around her own. 'Come and lie next to me,' he
commanded.

Uncomfortably, Rio slid up to him. He pulled her the
last few inches, until she was tight up against his hard body,
face to face in the dark.

His lean, sinewy thigh pushed between her own, sliding
up to thrust hard against her loins. That was too much. She
struggled in panicky outrage, but he was far too strong.

'Don't be a bloody fool,' he growled in her ear.

Her palms were flat against his chest, and she felt the
iron-hard muscles ripple under her fingers as he looped a
sheet round her waist, and tied her against him. The
intimacy of the contact was deeply disturbing. She lay still,
but stiffly rigid, acutely aware of his warmth against her, of
that hard thigh so intimately pressed between her legs,
against her woman's body. She could feel the caress of his
breath in her hair, smell the musk of his skin.

'There,' he said huskily, dragging the mattress up against
her back. 'This is cosy, isn't it?'

She said nothing, her heart pounding so hard that she
knew he must be able to feel its beat, and guess at how much
this contact was disconcerting her.

'Why did you come?' she said at last, her voice as stiff as
her body.

'I was worried about you,' he replied easily, pulling the
mattress into place. 'And I didn't think you'd survive
without me.'

'You took a chance with your own life,' she said quietly.

'I think I was more at risk from my driving than from
Trixie,' he observed wryly. 'I got that cut on the head from
a stone that smashed the windscreen. The coast roads aren't
meant for speeds above sixty.'

'No,' she agreed awkwardly. She'd never been very good
at expressing her thanks, even to those she loved. With this
man, whose effect on her life had been so ambiguous, she
was even more inhibited than usual. While she was still

picking and rejecting the words to use, she felt his hand caress her tangled blonde hair, and then the warm touch of a kiss on her brow.

'Beautiful Rio,' he said softly. 'You're as stiff as a board. Does it normally take a cyclone to get you into a man's arms?'

Hotly, she relaxed her muscles a millimetre, but didn't answer his gibe. The sudden buffet of wind swept a handful of sand across them, and Rio heard something creak in the house up above them.

'It'll come back very suddenly,' he warned, all humour gone from his voice now. 'Any time now. There's going to be a lot of sand and dust in here, little one. Cover your face against my chest.'

Another buffet of wind, stronger now, ended her hesitation. She could hear the terrifyingly familiar roar of Trixie's voice in the far distance now. With uninhibited urgency, she squeezed her arms out from between her body and his, and hugged him tight. His waist was hard and lean in her arms, the supple muscles taut with male power.

Sand was whipping around them, and small objects had started to skitter nervously across the ground. Rio pressed her face against the naked skin at the base of his throat, and Cameron tugged the lapels of his anorak around her cheeks, one muscular arm sheltering her head, the other protectively round her shoulders.

Numbly, she heard the rising sound of the wind outside their shelter. She squeezed her eyes shut in dread. She could taste the salt of his skin against her lips, could feel the strong, regular pulse of the big vein in his throat against her cheek. He said something briefly. She could make out only a deep rumble, but knew it was a message of comfort. She thanked God for his presence, huddling closer into the enclave of his arms, like a bird in the secure branches of an oak.

As if responding, his arms tightened, and she felt him press his own mouth against the wet, tangled hair on the top of her head.

Trixie exploded with a terrifying roar around the cottage, the whirling winds scything under the house like some vast threshing machine. The onslaught was as unbelievably violent as it had been before, the noise booming with added volume under the floorboards of the house. She clung to Cameron, cowering from the blast of sand and debris that found its way past the mattress, listening to the grotesque anger of a world gone mad.

There was no longer any embarrassment in the fact that they lay like lovers. Now she was grateful to her soul that he'd come, grateful for the comfort and protection of his body.

This time, the immense noise of the cyclone had a vicious note to it, as though resentful that its prey lay hidden beneath the house. Dull sounds in the great noise testified to the continuing destruction up above of whatever had survived the first onslaught. Now and then, Rio felt something slam into the mattress that protected her back, and she whimpered against Cameron's chest. Fear clawed at her nerves with added force now; she'd seen what the wind could do, knew with crueller clarity exactly what danger they were in. The floorboards above them creaked and vibrated, but seemed so far to be holding firm.

Endurance was all. She tried to shut her ears to the terrible storm, and fixed her senses on the most important thing in her world, the man in whose arms she lay. If she concentrated on the purely physical sensations of his arms locked round her, of his hot skin against her face, the menace of Trixie's all-devouring hatred seemed to fade.

Cameron's strength was rocklike, unyielding. She could feel his heart thudding against her, its steady beat accelerated, and the warmth of his breathing in her hair. Under her gripping fingers, the muscles of his back were taut.

Like lovers, she thought numbly. Like lovers sharing warmth in the dark, dark night. Concentrating on that thought hard enough brought on a kind of trance, a kind of inner peace. She clung to it mentally, as she clung to

Cameron physically, time fusing into one seamless, endless moment.

It was the sensation of icy cold that brought her out of it. There seemed to be a new noise in the storm, accompanied by a presence that licked along her side coldly. Rio twisted slightly in weary puzzlement, drawing her face back from his warm skin.

As she did so, an icy flood burst between their bodies, splashing into her face, and she choked on something that was salt in a very different way from the salt of Cameron's skin. For a moment, her mind couldn't grasp which element it was. Then, she registered that it was water.

The sea.

The sea was rising, had already flooded the beach, was starting to flood the underneath of the cottage.

A terrified panic surged into her, making her claw away from him, intent only on escaping from the horror of drowning there, in the dark, like a trapped rat.

His arms jerked her back with fierce strength, slamming her body against his.

'We've got to get *out*!' she screamed, her voice little more than a faint whisper in the roar of the wind.

'*No.*' Rio felt the word, rather than heard him shout it.

'The sea's—rising!' she screamed, pressing her mouth against his ear. 'We're going to—drown!'

'We're safe here.' The muscles of his chest surged with the effort of projecting his voice to her. 'We'll be—killed—out there——'

Sea water hit them in a torrent, drowning out his words. Rio screamed again in fear, hugging herself to him. 'Please,' she whimpered, hopelessly below the threshold of hearing. 'Let's get out of here!'

'There's nowhere—to go,' he shouted, trapping her against him. 'For God's sake—just—lie still!'

The water cut the sand away from beneath them in a vicious swipe, and she felt their bodies subside into the mud slightly. They were both soaked. Rio choking on wet sand she'd swallowed. She was too weak to struggle any further,

her store of energy having expended itself in that one abortive attempt to escape.

With a wave of complete surrender to Cameron's will, she pressed her face back against his smooth, wet skin. If they were going to die, she prayed dully, then let it be quick.

The water surged around them, rising perceptibly as the wind hurled it higher and higher up the land. With a shudder, she felt something flopping at her back, a frantic body slapping against her; and then the next wave flooded in, and it vanished. With an exhausted mind, Rio groped after that Cameron-trance again, trying to find the peace that grew out of not thinking about anything except him.

She was shivering in the cold and wet, and her whole body felt gritty with sand. Ignore it, she told herself savagely. It's not real. Only this is real, this embrace that's saving us both . . .

Time dragged by with a torturer's slow pace, then started to flow smoothly, then imperceptibly melted into that inner tranquillity she'd fought so hard to attain.

Time passed.

Far away, she was aware of Cameron's voice. She stirred herself, her fingers sliding across his wet skin. She'd torn his shirt some time during the storm, and her hands were tangled in the material, her watch catching on threads and snagging them.

'Rio!' He shook her gently. 'Wake up. Wake up!'

She squirmed in the mud, tried to sit upright, and banged her head sharply against the floorboards, making stars jump before her eyes.

'Ow!' She let him take her in his arms, her mind still only half-awake. 'Wha—what's happening?'

'It's all over.' He laughed softly. 'Trixie's passed!'

She listened, motionless. The only sound in the vast stillness was the long-drawn murmur of the surf, far away. There was dim light under the house, too, and a faint shimmer of reflected water on the boards above them.'

'Let's get out of here,' he said gently. 'You go first.'

'God!' She slithered in the direction he was pushing her, groping in the wet sand, towards the square of blue light ahead. They'd come through. Together, they'd survived.

She dragged herself through the hole, and squinted painfully in the piercing light, too cramped to get off her hands and knees.

Cameron emerged behind her, and helped her upright with gentle hands.

'Look,' he said in a tender voice, prising her protective fingers away from her eyes.

She couldn't see properly, but she could feel the heat of the sun on her skin. When she could open her eyes, she stared dazedly at the clear blue sky overhead. It was a beautiful day. The sea down below was blue.

She took it all in, the smashed palm trees, the earth that was strewn with trash and seaweed and dead fish, the roofless shell of the cottage, and then looked up at Cameron.

'Is it real?' she whispered.

He just smiled. Like her, he was filthy, his black curls clotted with sand. But the animal beauty of the dark blue eyes was undimmed, that aura of assured power unlessened. He reached out to brush the hair away from her face. Sand and dirt had turned it from platinum-pure to tawny. 'Yes,' he said gently, 'it's real.'

'It won't come back?' she asked.

'No. It won't come back.'

Laughing, she hugged him with an impulse of sheer delight, and he lifted her easily off the ground, letting her kick her heels up backwards.

Their kiss was as spontaneous as breathing, their mouths locking together with exuberant warmth.

'You're a brave lady,' he said softly, looking into her eyes. 'In fact, you're rather wonderful. Shall we see if there's anyone else left alive in the world?'

CHAPTER FOUR

THIS time, rigging up the radio set had been much easier. Between them, they'd agreed that it was pointless leaving the cottage yet.

'We'll try to assess the damage to the property and vehicles,' Cameron radioed to the coastguard, 'and salvage what we can from the house. There shouldn't be too much trouble fixing up some kind of sleeping arrangement overnight. We'll take it from there.'

'A coastguard launch will be working in your area tomorrow afternoon,' came the reply. 'It'll call by in the morning. If you want to be taken off then, there'll be room. Is there anything you particularly need, RX 105? Over.'

Cameron read out the list he and Rio had compiled, including fresh vegetables.

'We'll do our best to get that lot to you. Stay in touch,' the coastguard warned as he signed off, 'continuing storms and bad weather are likely over the next few days. Take care. Over and out.'

Rio had been poking through the wreckage disconsolately while he'd been using the radio, trying to find enough of her possessions to put into a pile. Now she peered through the shattered window at him, her expression tragic.

'Everything's gone,' she sighed. 'My books, my clothes, everything. Even my passport. And all that's left of my work is the bare records.' Her grey eyes filled with tears. 'I'm *destitute*. What am I going to do?'

He smiled compassionately at her misery. 'We'll work something out,' he promised.

'It's all scattered,' she said, shaking her head. 'I could never have believed anything natural could be so ——' She groped for a word. 'So *malevolent*.' She shook her tousled head. 'Trixie's such a damned banal name. Why do cyclones have to be feminine?'

'They don't.' He put the cover over the short-wave set. 'The Aborigines call the cyclone *Jangawal*. The Thunder Man. They say he comes to punish those who harm his people.'

'But I haven't harmed anyone,' said Rio in a little voice. 'And look what your Thunder Man's done to me . . .'

He looked at her for a moment, then rose to his feet. 'Come on,' he said comfortingly, 'let's go and find my jeep.'

Stiff with the cramped hours under the house, Rio climbed down, and walked with him down the littered track. 'Driving here must have been terrible,' she said. 'Were you afraid?'

'Terrified,' he smiled. 'As soon as I got the news that Trixie had changed direction, I set off from Barramundi. The storm hit me about twenty miles up the coast, near the river, just when I thought I was going to make it in time. A big gust blew me right off the road, but fortunately it didn't overturn the jeep.'

'What did you do,' she asked in horror.

'I found some animal's hole in the bank,' he said calmly. 'I used the shovel from the jeep to dig it wide enough to shelter inside. By that time, Trixie was starting to snap trees in half, so I just squeezed myself in, and waited for it to blow over.'

That explained his battered appearance, she thought with awe. 'I don't think that would have occurred to me,' she said in a small voice. 'I'd have just been blown away.'

'That's why I came.'

'I'm very glad that you did.' With a feeling of real warmth, she snuggled up to his side, laying her blonde head on his shoulder. 'I don't know how I would have made it through those last hours without you.'

If it occurred to him that her behaviour towards him had changed dramatically since the cyclone, he didn't comment.

A few hundred yards further on, they came upon a group of palm trees collapsed across the road. Beyond that, Cameron's red jeep was in a ditch, nose-first. The cyclone had blasted it with rocks and debris, the bodywork was badly dented, and the windscreen missing completely, but as Cameron climbed on a trunk to get a better viewpoint he grunted in satisfaction.

'Should be able to get her out,' he judged.

'Can I help?' she offered.

'You just relax,' he smiled. 'I'll have to get this lot out of the way before we can go anywhere.'

Rio perched on the dusty edge of the road, basking in the sun, and watched while Cameron lowered his tall frame over the jammed door and into the driver's seat. The engine fired easily, then rose to a howl as he gunned the throttle. In a spray of gravel the jeep clawed itself backwards, and up on to the road. He jumped out, leaving the engine running, and tied a towrope to the first of the fallen trees.

It took him half an hour to clear the road. Rio watched the economical power of his movements, the consummate skill with which he handled the four-wheel-drive vehicle and the heavy workload. Just the man to be shipwrecked on a desert island with, she thought dreamily. His competence and energy were phenomenal.

But for his presence here, she might well be dead by now. What a strange meeting it had been, in that weird calm Eye. She thought of that shadow in the wave again. Maybe it had been a dolphin, after all.

Driving back to the cottage, the wind blowing through the glassless frame of the windscreen, Cameron brought up the subject of her immediate future.

'What are your plans?' he asked. 'To head back to England?'

'No,' she said firmly, clinging to the jolting dashboard. 'I'm going to stay, and get my work done.'

'Where?'

'I haven't thought yet,' she confessed.

'I don't know what condition Barramundi's in,' he said, 'but it's very much more sheltered on that part of the coast, and the old house has withstood more than one cyclone in the past two centuries. Besides which, my staff will be taking care of any damage. You obviously can't stay at the cottage, and even if you could it'll be days before the sea's clear enough for you to dive, and check the condition of the reef.' He pulled up next to the house, and turned to her, 'My suggestion is that you come to Barramundi, and stay with me for the next couple of weeks. That way you can get your report written up, and still be within a reasonable distance of your subjects.'

It was an unexpected idea, and one that had distinct advantages. 'You're very kind,' she said slowly. 'But it would be an awful bother for you . . .'

'No, it wouldn't,' he replied with a slight smile, and met her eyes. 'I'd like to have you there, Rio.'

Was there a shade of warmth in those deep blue eyes—something that went beyond the simple, polite hospitality of a colleague? She thought hard, weighing up the attractions. The only feasible alternative was to go back to Brisbane, four hundred miles away, and ask the Cotton Foundation Liaison Office to try and find her some other place. An uncertain and very long-drawn-out option. 'Thank you,' she said at last. 'It's a very generous offer. But——'

'Think it over.' He forestalled any further discussion by climbing out of the jeep. 'There's a hell of a lot to do, and nobody but us to do it. First of all, I'd better try and find the Land Rover. Why don't you round up as many of your things as you can find in the meantime? You'll have to do that, whatever you decide to do.'

Rio nodded, and moved to obey him.

By late afternoon, she'd assembled a small pile of clothes and books, all that was left of the kit she'd left London with two months ago. It wasn't much, but at least she would have something to wear for the next few days.

Using the jeep, Cameron had managed to drag the Land Rover out of the water, and up on to the highest part of the beach. Despite having attempted to dry the electrics, it wasn't starting, and eventually he gave up in disgust.

'I'm starving,' he announced, coming back to the cottage.

'So am I,' she nodded, then glanced at him warily, the

taste of that steak still haunting her conscience.

'There's still some meat left,' he said calmly, nodding at the rucksack.

Her expression turned mutinous, and he sighed resignedly.

'OK, Rio, OK. If I got you a fish, by any remote chance, would you stoop to eat it?'

'It would be marginally less unacceptable,' she said shortly.

He turned without a word, and went to the jeep. He returned, carrying a magnificent silver-blue fish about a yard long. 'It swam too close while I was fastening the rope to your Land Rover,' he said casually, and with a flinch she saw the clean gash in its side where he'd harpooned it.

'God,' she said quietly, staring with distaste at the dead creature, 'you really enjoy the pioneering life, don't you? I bet you haven't had as much fun since the last cyclone!'

'Everything on the planet lives by the death of other creatures,' he said with a glint in his eyes that might have been amusement at her naïveté or anger at her rebuke—or maybe both. 'And that includes you. I find it an artificial distinction to differentiate between a living fish and a living turnip.'

'The turnip doesn't feel pain,' she retorted briskly.

'Got any proof of that?' he enquired drily, arching one dark eyebrow.

'No,' she said, moving into the familiar rhythm of an argument she knew from countless university discussions, 'but we have to go on empirical evidence and, as far as science has been able to determine, the nervous system of vegetables is far cruder than that of even the simplest animal life-form.'

'You sound as though you're at some Oxford debate,' he said with amused contempt. 'Merton College, if I'm not wrong. Is that where you picked your vegetarianism up?'

'I didn't *pick it up*,' she said coldly. 'It's not some kind of illness! It's a principle which happens to be deeply important to me. I don't take life unless it's strictly necessary.'

'Bravo,' he said with gentle irony. 'That doesn't make you any better than this fish. I presume it would offend your deeply held principles to scale and clean it?'

'I wouldn't know where to begin,' she shuddered.

'Of course not,' he said with a dry smile. 'Then I'll allow you to restrict your contribution to this massacre of the innocents to building another fire.' With that smooth economy of movement, he squatted on his hunkers, and started gutting the fish with a knife.

Averting her gaze, Rio went to gather firewood. Her mind was turning over angry retorts and arguments to pierce that massive male self-composure of his. She made the fire, then wandered restlessly back to Cameron. Though she hardly wanted to witness what he was doing, she couldn't leave the argument where it had been laid down.

'You think vegetarianism's a feeble philosophy, don't you?' she challenged, standing at his shoulder.

'Each to his own,' he said without looking up.

'Why can't you accept that people can live without killing or exploiting animals?' she asked bitterly.

'You're a funny sort of biologist,' he smiled, starting to scale the bullet-smooth fish. 'Hasn't it dawned on you that the entire cycle of existence is based on creatures killing and exploiting each other?'

'That's a horrible view of the world!'

'Nonsense,' he retorted. 'It's accurate.'

'But humans should be above that,' she argued fiercely. 'It's our duty to rise *above* our animal origins!'

'No,' he said with quiet intensity. 'It's our duty to understand and accept our own humanity, Rio. Not to try and raise ourselves on some glittering pedestal above other life on this planet. You can call that Frazer's Law.'

'You don't believe in the laws of evolution, I take it?' she snapped.

'I believe that the further we leave what you call "our

animal origins" behind us, the worse off we are.' He looked
up at her with eyes that had caught the wild blue of the late
afternoon sky. 'Yes, I enjoy living in harmony with nature,'
he said quietly. 'But, unlike you, I don't prate or preach
about it. And unlike you, the idea of killing—or being
killed—doesn't fill me with holy terror.'

'I can't help being frightened of dying,' she said in a hurt
voice, remembering her misery during the cyclone.

'You were very brave, as a matter of fact,' he said, that
wonderful smile breaking through the grimness of his
expression. 'But the Foundation which finances your
current research is all about bringing man and nature into
harmony, Rio. That's what old Jesse Cotton learned, and
that's what he wanted others to learn. You should be trying
to learn, and teach, that same lesson.' He held out the
cleaned fish to her. 'Will you take this down to the sea and
wash it?' he asked calmly.

Rio took the smooth body with distaste, and went down
to obey him. She was definitely having second thoughts
about that invitation to Barramundi.

He cooked it over the embers, the exquisite aroma
making up for her earlier struggle of conscience. It was so
easy, she thought, feeling her stomach churn in anticipation of food, to slip from the straight and narrow path of
vegetarianism. She studied Cameron's face through the curl
of fragrant blue smoke. He was, she was just beginning to
realise, the most beautiful male she'd ever seen. Not just
handsome and well made, but burning with an inner power
and vitality that was unforgettable.

She watched his hands, assessing the combination of
strength and grace in them. The best sort of hands,
competent and yet gentle. Hands to kill a fish, repair a
broken radio, hands to love a woman . . .

How much he was missing, she thought with sudden
realisation. A man with his intelligence and energy could
achieve a great deal in society. Could have as many
beautiful women as he wanted, as much money and success
as he could deal with. Could carve himself a very tempting

piece of that vast merry-go-round called the world.

And yet, here he was, on a remote shore, with no apparent ambition beyond discovering some dark principle of a shark's mind.

Odd? Or, perhaps, more like her than she acknowledged?

Sharks. Magnificent creatures, but deadly and destructive creatures, too. Was it because of them that his view of life was so brutally simple? Or had that acceptance of the dangerous side of life actually drawn him towards animals so uniquely and frighteningly adapted to the process of survival?

'It's rude to stare,' he said gently, and she realised with a hot flush that she was looking straight into his eyes.

'I was miles away,' Rio blushed.

'I could see that,' he smiled, and passed over a piece of fish. It was deliciously succulent and hot, and she ate with relish, not caring whether there was an ironic smile on his face or not.

'Where are we going to sleep tonight?' she asked later, accepting the second helping he offered.

'The back seat of the jeep folds down,' he suggested. 'We could rig up some blankets . . .'

She glanced at the jeep, thinking with unease of the intimacy that arrangement would entail. The prospect of curling up with Cameron Frazer all over again was somewhat unsettling; but if he followed her eyes, and guessed at the way her heart was sinking, he made no sign.

Unless that slight smile on his lips had something to do with it.

They kept the fire going as the sun began to set, piling logs on to it until it blazed and crackled. The first stars came out in a cloudless evening sky, dazzling as diamonds. The smell of woodsmoke and the tang of sea-salt on the air blended into a haunting perfume that Rio knew she'd remember for the rest of her life.

'I thought I was living really close to nature here,' she

murmured, hugging her knees and staring into the red depths of the flames. 'But I was still caught between four walls. If Trixie's done nothing else, at least she's blown those walls down. I'd forgotten what it was really like to be out in the open . . .'

'Most people have.' He brought her a blanket, and draped it round her shoulders. She snuggled into it, smiling her thanks. Cameron sprawled beside her in catlike relaxation. 'You don't strike me as having led a sheltered life, though,' he said. 'You were orphaned, weren't you, and brought up by an elderly aunt in Brisbane?'

'You seem to know a lot about me,' she said, glancing at him over her shoulder.

'I had a long letter about you from someone on some committee in London. As a senior colleague, I was asked whether I would keep an eye on you. I replied that I'd do so, but somehow . . .' He shrugged. 'I was stupidly wrapped up in my own work. It doesn't matter now. How did your parents die?'

'In a car crash,' she said, brooding into the flames. 'I was twelve.'

'Was there no one except your aunt to take you?'

Rio shook her head. 'They put me in a foster home for nine months, but I couldn't stand it.' She told him how she'd written to Maudie, and how Maudie had flown out to rescue her.

'She must have been a remarkable woman,' he said thoughtfully.

'Oh, she was. She was a really gifted naturalist, completely self-taught. There wasn't much she didn't know about birds or plants.' She found herself telling him about her life with Maudie, about the holiday journeys—they'd called them 'field trips'—which the two of them had taken all over Australia, observing, collecting, learning. The unforgettable holiday at Ayer's Rock, the giant red heart of the Australian continent, and most sacred of all the Aboriginal Dreamtime sites; trips to the eastern mountains, to the lowland plains of the coast, to the vast inland deserts where the salt lakes shimmered in terrible heat. Cameron listened in deep silence, while she told him how her love of nature had grown and deepened—though whether he was taking it in attentively, or simply letting her ramble over his own inner thoughts, she didn't know.

'Maudie was a vegetarian,' she finished, huddling into her blanket as she noticed how dark and cool it had become. 'There was no way I could give up meat at boarding-school, because they just didn't cater for that kind of thing. But while I was at Oxford, I joined the vegetarian society——'

'You can eat what you please at Barrimundi,' he said gently. 'The chef will cook whatever you ask for. I really don't care, Rio. Don't make such a thing of it.'

Rio sat in silence, wondering exactly what life was going to be like at Barramundi. *My staff. The chef.* If nothing else, it sounded intriguingly luxurious!

But there was something about Cameron Frazer, the way he got to her, maybe, that was very disquieting. It might not be such a good idea to stay with him, after all. He was a man it would be all too easy to become obsessive about. Obsessive, possessive, a lot of things she didn't want to be at this stage of her life.

And she—she would never be anything to him. Anything more than an amusing waif. Or maybe an irritating one. But nothing serious, ever.

'What's Barramundi like?' she asked, coming out of her thoughts, and poking the fire with a stick.

'Very quiet,' he said, with an odd hint of a smile in his deep voice.

She waited for more, and when none came, echoed, 'Quiet? Is that all?'

'No, that's not all,' he said. 'It's also very beautiful.'

'And lonely?' suggested Rio, glancing at his big, dark shape beside her.

'Loneliest place on earth,' he said calmly.

'Despite all your staff?' she hinted.

'Despite the staff,' he half smiled. 'They're wonderful people, mostly Filipinos. But when I say it's lonely, I mean that it's lonely by choice. Any place can be lonely or crowded, according to your own choice. And I choose to have Barramundi lonely.'

'And you've already been there almost three months,' she mused, wishing she could see more of his face than a harshly carved profile against the flames. 'How much longer before your research is finished?'

'That's impossible to say.'

'You've already spent months,' she said, her voice lifting, 'in the loneliest place on earth. God, you must get bored!'

'No more than you. Besides, I keep myself busy,' he said, again giving that hint of an inner smile.

'It's hard to imagine how—apart from your research,' she said, not quite digging, yet making it clear she wanted an answer of some kind from him.

'Oh . . .' He lay back, clasping his hands behind his head. 'I get to town now and then. People come to see me sometimes.'

'Women?' she asked, her voice coming out unexpectedly sharply.

'Now,' he said gently, 'what is this? An interrogation?'

'You've been asking about *my* family history for the past hour,' she said in an aggrieved tone.

'No,' he corrected coolly, 'I asked you two questions, and you've talked until the stars came out.'

Rio sat in silence, damning him—and her stupid self for walking into that one. 'Well, I'm sorry if I've been boring you,' she said shortly, and tossed her stick into the fire. 'You should have stopped me.'

He rolled over, like a huge cat, and smiled up at her, the firelight etching his stubbly cheeks. 'Don't be so prickly,' he reproved.

'You're the one who's prickly,' she retorted. 'I just wanted to know a little about you, but you obviously prefer to remain enigmatic. Or maybe you just don't like me.'

'I do like you.' His eyes stayed on hers, the firelight reflected in each glowing pupil. 'And you'll have plenty of time to find out about me—and Barramundi—when we get there.'

'Magical mystery tour?' she suggested acidly, still stiff-necked at the snub she was sure—or *almost* sure—he'd just given her. 'Is that it?'

'No,' he said patiently, 'that's not it. But there are certain relationships which one shouldn't rush.'

Completely floored, Rio could only stare at him in silence, until something popped in the fire, sending sparks skittering upwards, and making her jump nervously. 'What sort of relationships?' she asked.

'Relationships like this one.'

'I don't know what sort of relationship this one is,' Rio said, suddenly becoming aware that she was on very shaky ground with this man, that they were a long way from anywhere, and that there was something dizzingly mesmeric about that firelit stare of his. 'You're a scientist, I'm a scientist, you came to my rescue during a cyclone. What else can there be?'

'That,' he said with amused logic, 'is what we have to find out. Slowly. The way you should always explore a relationship that promises great richness.' He paused slightly. 'Like conducting an important experiment. Or like making love to someone for the first time.'

Rio felt her heart flip over inside her chest. 'Is that why you invited me to Barramundi?' she asked nervously. 'To——' She hesitated. 'To explore a relationship?'

'I invited you because you just don't have anywhere else to go. And because you're a fellow scientist, and I somehow feel responsible for you. But also because I get the feeling that if I were to let you run back to London, you would haunt me.'

'I'm going to get some more wood,' Rio said briskly, and hoisted herself up, clutching her blanket around her for warmth as she went in search of driftwood that was scarcely needed. Haunt? Run? Words that had come out casually, yet which had been chosen with disturbing care. Damn him! He was telling her something, yet she didn't know what, didn't even know how to react, because she didn't know what he meant.

She went down to the sea's edge, and washed her hands and face in the cold water, suddenly feeling how tired she was. Trixie had worn her out. It really wasn't her fault that she was jumpy and on edge tonight. *Haunt.* What did he mean?

The trouble was that she hadn't spoken plainly to him. She'd fenced and parried with him, and he was a damn sight deadlier a fencer and parrier than she was.

She scooped up five or six decent-sized sticks of wood, and armed with that, went back to the fire. He was lying where she'd left him, long, lean legs stretched comfortably out to the blaze. She piled the wood on to the fire, and it blazed up brightly, flaring heat out at them.

'That'll burn all night,' Cameron said approvingly. 'We'd better turn in for the night, now. It's been a very long day.'

Ready as she was for a great deal more talk, Rio bit her lip. But she held her peace. Weariness was creeping along her limbs, that ache that told her she'd overstretched her muscles, and needed rest. Every time she talked to Cameron, he seemed to sting her somewhere, leave her prickling and unsatisfied. Did he mean to frustrate her like this? There was probably very little he did, she realised grimly, that he didn't mean to do.

In the glimmer of the bonfire, she watched him pile blankets, clothes and pillows into the back of the jeep, making an inelegant but very cosy-looking bed. A double bed.

He pulled the jeep's canvas hood into position. It was battered, but still serviceable.

'We both smell pretty smoky and fishy.' He smiled at her. 'And sandy and salty too, I guess. But I won't complain if you won't.'

Rio hesitated as he held the door open for her. She'd resolved to be frank with him. 'It occurs to me,' she said slowly, 'that a man might get rather short of female

company in three months at Barramundi. By *company*, I
mean . . .'

'You mean sex,' he said calmly.

'Yes,' she nodded, her face elfin, yet serious, in the orange
light.

'And you think I want you at Barramundi in order to
slake my pent-up desires on your admittedly very desirable
body,' he said drily, leaning on the door and watching her
with dark eyes.

'Something like that,' she nodded again, huddling into
her blanket like a squaw in front of a strange brave's
wigwam.

He tilted his head back, surveying her from under level
black eyebrows. 'Would it upset you if that *was* what I
wanted?' he enquired.

'Of course it would!' she said stiffly.

'Why?' he asked. 'Plenty of women might be glad of an
offer like that.'

'Oh, you! You think too damned much of yourself!' she
snapped furiously, then saw that he was laughing at her.

'Come on, Rio,' he said softly. 'I'm just teasing you. Let's
get some sleep.'

She woke near dawn, her head pillowed on Cameron's
chest, her body huddled close up to his. She could hear the
patter of rain on the canvas hood, the hiss of drops among
the embers of the fire.

About falling asleep last night she remembered nothing.
She'd simply clambered in with Cameron, had let him take
her in his arms, and had been asleep in seconds.

Strange intimacy, she thought dreamily, to be so closely
snuggled up to this hard, warm, alien body. His breathing
was deep and even, his arms locked around her
protectively.

It would be so very easy to call it love. So easy to let her
imagination identify his embrace as passion, desire,
possession.

It was a long, long time since she'd lain with a man. Not

since Oxford, almost a year ago. And no man had ever held her like this, with such protection, such strength. They'd sprawled beside her, close, yet coldly separate. Without real contact. With Cameron there was a unity, a oneness that was very new to her. And yet achingly familiar. Or was that, too, her imagination?

She disentangled her hands from where they'd been clasped between her breasts, and laid her palm with infinite lightness on his chest. Beneath the hard muscles, she could feel his heart beating steadily and powerfully.

Fragments of last night's talk drifted through her thoughts. He hadn't really answered her question about Barramundi. Had he said he desired her? Or had he just been teasing her, enjoying her nervous reactions to his hints? Barramundi was taking on a kind of mystical significance in her imaginings now, an importance far out of proportion to a simple invitation, a simple visit.

Should she go? Or should she ask the coastguards to take her back to Brisbane, and maybe resign herself to the possibility that she would never get her report written up?

No. She was far too committed to her work now. It would hurt like mad to simply write off those weeks of monitoring, testing and sampling. Barramundi was by far the best idea, especially since she'd be within easy reach of the reef, and could add those final, vital measurements, giving her research an added depth and meaning.

Besides which, the idea of being waited on by a beaming Filipino staff had distinct attractions, even to someone as austere in her habits as Rio Faber.

The thorn beneath the rose was Cameron Frazer. She didn't dare examine her own emotions as regarded him. Rio had never thought of herself as particularly vulnerable before; but with Cameron she was unbelievably open, susceptible to every word or look. It was a time to be very, very careful.

Yes, she would go with him to Barramundi, accepting that unusually generous offer from a comparative stranger. But she would go on her own terms, not on his. And she would remember, all the time, that she would be walking a very thin tightrope . . .

She felt Cameron stir slightly. His hand slid up her back, caressing the salt-stiff tumble of her tawny hair.

'What are you thinking about?' he murmured, his breath warm against her cheek.

'I didn't know you were awake,' she said. Then, guiltily, withdrew her outspread hand from his chest. 'Did I wake you?'

'No, the rain did.'

'It woke me, too. There, it's stopped now.' Suddenly, she was very conscious of their closeness, and very wide awake. 'It's so quiet,' she whispered.

'The birds haven't woken up yet.' He drew her close with powerful arms, rumbling deep in his throat with satisfaction, like a great cat. 'Hmmm, you're warm. And you smell so good.'

'Of *Chanel Number Five*?' she asked, using irony to cover the way her heart had begun to pound.

'No,' he said huskily. 'Of woman's hair and warm woman's skin. Better than any perfume.' She closed her eyes as she felt his lips caress her temple, their velvety heat moving down her cheek in a chain made of slow, light kisses. 'I shall miss this smell when you start using soap and powder,' he murmured.

'You won't get close enough to me to be able to tell,' she assured him. But her lips were dry, her throat constricted with nerves.

'Won't I?' Cameron's lips savoured the texture of her skin, brushing to and fro across the satin-smooth area dangerously close to her mouth.

'Besides,' she said, her voice just a dry whisper, 'you wouldn't really want me to smell like a savage all the time . . . would you?' Cameron didn't answer; he was teasing the corner of her mouth, kissing gently yet insistently at the point where the skin became soft and sensitive.

Rio turned her head aside hotly, afraid of the sharp rush of excitement his kiss was sending through her veins. But he took her chin in his fingers and pulled her gently back to face him.

'Are you afraid of me?' he asked quietly.

'Yes,' she whispered, too emotional to hide the truth at that moment. In the warm darkness, with the smell of woodsmoke and fresh rain still on the air, she was a long, long way from civilisation. 'Terrified.'

'Why?'

'I don't know . . .'

This time he kissed her full on the lips, covering her mouth with a gentle firmness that stopped any hesitation on her part. She tried to lie rigid in his arms, unresponding, in silent protest, but the gentle pressure of his mouth was easing her own lips apart, exposing the moist inner warmth to his exploring tongue.

It was like a kind of exquisite torture to lie motionless while his tongue traced the line of her lips, the caress devastatingly sensual, intimate beyond even the act of love itself. His fingers were roaming through her hair, pressing her face to his so that she had no escape. Her lips, which had been so dry and unwelcoming, had suddenly became damp and soft, clinging to his. And that male tongue was touching her teeth, probing gently yet insistently for entry.

She could not bear it any longer. With a tiny whimper, she unclenched her teeth, accepting the entrance of his tongue. It sent her pulses rocketing, her veins flooded with intoxication, to feel it meet her own, slippery and pointed and firm where her own tongue was timid and yielding. Suddenly Rio's pleasure-centres were aching fiercely, and she strained her slim body to his, as though wanting to press them against his hard body, desperate for the satisfaction of his touch, even through the clothes they wore.

But instead of the deep, thrusting kiss she abruptly hungered for, his mouth teased gently, with intolerable sweetness, and then withdrew. As if oblivious to the fact that he had set her on fire from head to foot, he sighed contentedly, kissing the dewy skin of her eyelids.

'Go back to sleep,' he purred, shifting so that her head

was pillowed on his shoulder again. 'It's not even dawn yet.'

Rio almost groaned aloud in frustration. He was doing it again, arousing her passions with a wickedly cruel expertise, then sliding away just as she was about to commit herself.

She lay in his arms, dismally aware of her own arousal, feeling how ready her body was for him. Nothing any man had ever done to her had achieved the arousal Cameron had provoked in that seemingly casual kiss. She found herself grinding her teeth, every touch of her clothes against her breasts and loins a torment. What had he done *this* for? Just to make a fool of her? She could almost have scratched his face with angry claws, to wipe that Cheshire-cat smile of his away.

'I lost my virginity in the back of a car,' he mused, as if it were the most inconsequential thing in the world to say. 'Or don't men have a virginity to lose?'

'I don't know whether they do or not,' she said through clenched teeth. 'But I find it very hard to believe that *you* ever had a virginity to lose, Mr Frazer.'

She felt the muscles of his cheek move in a quick smile against her own face. 'In any case,' he said softly, 'love is something one gains, not loses. Don't you agree?'

'I'm not very comfortable.' Grumpy and juvenile though it was, she got a mean satisfaction from twisting out of Cameron's arms and turning her back on him.

Undaunted, he snuggled up close to her back, arms closing around her to hold her close, his hands perilously close beneath her breasts. With an almost physical pain, she longed for him to hold them, like a lover.

But he wasn't a lover.

She heard his breathing become deep and slow. Real sleep or feigned? Probably real. Rio Faber wasn't exciting enough to keep him awake any longer, she thought bitterly. If she'd had the lush personality of a film starlet, instead of the prickly one God had given her, maybe he'd have stayed awake. And if she'd had the lush breasts of a starlet, maybe he'd have been tempted to hold them. But as it was . . .

He slept. And Rio lay in a grim, resentful silence, as if daring sleep to try anything on with *her*.

CHAPTER FIVE

THE rain had gone by morning, leaving the sun free reign to bake down on a recovering world. She awoke drowsily to see Cameron already up, and clearing away the remains of last night's fire.

'Good morning,' he smiled as she poked her tousled head out of the jeep's window. 'How do you feel?'

'Stiff and sore.' Rio clambered out, stretching herself in the morning warmth. 'And very dirty.'

He surveyed her assessingly. 'You look all three. How about a swim to start the day?'

She nodded eager assent to the deliciously tempting idea, and followed him down through the ravaged palm grove, and on to the beach. Even now, she was still trying to adjust to the miracle of their survival. With the extraordinary unpredictability of cyclone weather, Trixie had left a glorious day in her wake, a world cleansed of that ominous mugginess that had preceded her.

Trixie had also changed the contours of the sand completely, sculpting the little bay to her own design, and everything seemed different to Rio's wondering eyes.

At the edge of the water, Cameron started stripping off his clothes. Rio watched uncertainly as his brown, superbly muscled torso emerged from the dusty denims and anorak, then slowly started unpeeling her own clothes. No maidenly reserve could overcome her desperate need to wash the sand, and the memory of yesterday's near death, from her body.

Carefully avoiding even a glance at Cameron, she waded into the water with her panties still on, hugging her small, high breasts, and flopped gratefully into the lapping waves with a sigh of sheer pleasure.

She let herself simply sink into the turquoise water,
feeling the knots of her hair untangling slowly. When she
surfaced, shaking her hair back in a sunlit arc, Cameron
was swimming out towards her with an experienced
swimmer's easy crawl. She slipped off her panties, and
kicked out for deeper water, with a sheer, intense delight in
feeling the cool water between her thighs and around her
naked breasts.

He caught her up just where the water turned from cool
to cold, as the shelf beneath dropped away to bluer depths.
Treading water, she let him approach, his eyes reflecting
the profound colour of the sky.

'What time is it?' she panted.

'Who cares?' he smiled.

She laughed breathlessly. 'Who cares?' she echoed.
'We're alive!' She peered at the bruise on his forehead in
concern, noting the healing cut. 'Does that hurt?'

He grimaced. 'It's throbbing badly.'

'Is it?' She swam close, and reached up to touch the bruise
with careful fingers. But he'd been teasing her, and she
gasped as she felt strong arms imprison her, drawing her
close up against his nakedness. 'Traitor!' she gasped at his
perfidy. She tried to recoil from the contact with smooth,
naked muscle, but he simply grinned down at her, his
expression wickedly amused.

'You weren't quite so shy earlier this morning,' he said
softly.

'We had clothes on then,' Rio pointed out. She clung to
his powerful shoulders, and looked up, almost hypnotised
by his eyes. They were deep, warm. There was something
in them that both frightened her, and drew her potently.
Something that said he knew everything about a woman,
understood both passion and desire, knew her innermost
secrets.

'You're so beautiful,' he said softly, brooding on her
mouth as they floated in the cool swell. She felt his hard
man's nipples brush the soft peaks of her own breasts, his

lean thigh sliding warmly between hers. Without any consciousness of having allowed or avoided it, Rio's mouth was lifting for his kiss. It was fleeting, for as soon as his warm, wet lips claimed hers, her heart flipped over inside her. God! Let him not repeat last night's performance, with the added impact of their nudity on his side!

She squirmed out of his arms like an alarmed eel, and shot off towards the shore, escape the overriding idea in her mind.

When she looked over her shoulder, Cameron was swimming after her with the easy power of a pursuing cruiser. He was clearly as at home in the water as she was, his movements as sure and fluid as those of a big, compact fish. An odd mixture of anger, amusement, and panic took hold of her as it turned into a game of flight and pursuit—but a game that made her heart pound in her chest, nevertheless.

In the shallow water she turned again, but he was nowhere to be seen. She paused, and scanned the water with anxious grey eyes. Where the hell was he? The waves curled and creamed, glass walls glittering emptily against the sun, devoid of any sign of life. All her amusement started turning to panic as the long seconds ticked slowly by without a glimpse of him.

'Cameron?' She waded uncertainly outwards. '*Cameron*!' In the horrified thought that the treacherous undertow might have swept him under the blue-green water, her legs turned to jelly. She called his name again. He'd been under far too long for it to have been a joke. God! Had they survived the cyclone only for him to drown now?

Suddenly the water erupted in front of her, and she let out one short scream as his naked brown body surged up against hers, potent arms clamping round her waist, and lifting her effortlessly out of the water, waist-high into the sun.

'Bastard!' She pounded his shoulders with futile knuckles. 'Put me *down*.'

'You're rather too fond of that word.' His eyes glinted

dangerously as he looked up at his prisoner, taking in her angry face, the soft curve of two perfect breasts, the dark nipples hard with tension. 'It's not only insulting, but inaccurate. I can assure you that my antecedents are quite impeccable.'

He let her slide down against him, but did not release her. In fact, there was something in his expression which suggested that releasing her was the last thing on his mind right then.

'You frightened me,' she said defensively, avoiding his stare uncomfortably. 'I thought you'd drowned. I didn't mean to call you names.'

'You're always so cool and self-possessed,' said Cameron softly. 'No one would imagine you'd just been through a cyclone.'

'What am I expected to do?' Diamond-bright, her eyes challenged him with a confidence she was very far from feeling. 'Melt submissively into your arms?'

'You're in my arms already,' he pointed out silkily. 'But you're far from submissive.'

'You've probably saved my life,' she said, trying to back away from the hard, warm body that kept brushing against hers. 'I'd have died without you. But if you're expecting me to show my gratitude by——'

She broke off, warned by the subtle change in his eyes that hinted at anger.

'By—what?' he asked gently.

'We ought to go back to the cottage,' she pleaded, cursing her awkwardness with this dangerously attractive man. 'The coastguard will be here this morning, and we have to get ready to leave for Barramundi——'

His eyes glittered. 'Then you accept my invitation?'

'I don't have much choice, do I?' she asked, deliberately making it sound as graceless as possible.

'How very practical you are.' He kissed her flinching mouth lightly, resting his forehead against hers, and linking his hands behind her neck. 'Is there no romance at all in that cool little soul of yours?'

'We're both supposed to be scientists,' she said. But her mouth was dry, and the blood was surging along her veins with an emotion that was starting to grow wryly familiar to her. Fear or excitement, she could never tell which, but it stirred her innermost feelings. Maybe something in between.

'To be precise, we're both biologists,' he smiled. The black curls of his hair had been swept back, emphasising the harsh male beauty of his face. From a few inches away, she could see that his skin was flawless, the metallic sheen of his tan etched with the dark stubble of forty-eight hours' growth. He had lashes that were shamelessly long for a man's, and their dark shade made the level heat of that blue stare all the more distracting. 'And you seem remarkably blind to the biology evolving between us.' He kissed her temples with great care, making her close her eyes with an involuntary shiver of response. 'Which are you, Rio?' he murmured. 'Unobservant—or wilfully blind?'

'Nothing's evolving between us,' she said, her voice breathless. 'And I find it odd that at a time like this you should be thinking of—of sex!'

'Danger is a potent aphrodisiac. Hadn't you heard?'

'Not for me, it isn't!'

'Wilfully blind,' he said softly, and slanted his head to kiss her with a brutal male force that took utter possession of her. His mouth was hungry, demanding, and expert. She could only cling to him helplessly as his smooth tongue forced between her teeth, far more rough than he'd been last night.

His hands, too, were demanding as they caressed urgently up her flanks and across her ribs, cupping her neat breasts with a ruthless satisfaction that told her instinctively that it was something he'd ached to do from the moment he'd first set eyes on her.

She could not stop herself from responding to him. There was a growing need in her that dominated all other conscious thought. Her hands were feverish as they caressed the thick, wet tangle of his hair, urging him to kiss her harder, deeper; her breasts were unbearably conscious of his touch, the brush of his thumbs across her hard nipples giving her a rush of sensual release that at the same time opened the door to a swelling desire for more passion.

'Rio,' he whispered, kissing her arched-back throat, his hands moulding the sweet line of her hips, 'I want you . . .'

She was too full of emotion to speak. He slid an arm under her thighs, and lifted her up, wading to the shore with her in his arms, as though she were a child. The water poured from their naked bodies. He set her on her feet in the warm sand, smiling down at her with a mouth that had been carved by some pagan god for a woman's pleasure.

'How beautiful you are,' he said softly, his words almost lost in the murmur of the surf.

If he'd wanted to make love to her at that moment, Rio knew that she could not have resisted. She was his already, spellbound by him.

Her throat was dry and speechless as she looked at Cameron's nakedness. He was magnificently built, the muscled breadth of his chest covered with a broad triangle of black hair that trickled all the way down his flat belly to spread again with liberal potency at his loins. His was the body of a Greek god, kissed by the sun and hardened by relentless exercise. He had a horseman's lean and powerful legs, an athlete's deep-chested strength.

Beside him, her own body was slight, her unflawed golden skin marked only by the two stars of her breasts, the tiny flower of her navel, and the mysterious triangle of maiden-hair between her slender thighs.

Cameron took her water-beaded face in his hands, and kissed her wet mouth with tender reverence. 'Come on, practical Rio,' he said gently. 'Let's go and get ready to leave.'

Her legs were as weak as jelly, her stomach full of quivering butterflies, but he seemed unwilling to go any further with that kiss.

She had to tear her eyes away from him. They dressed in silence, Rio's soul in such a state of chaos that her fingers shook, making it difficult for her to put on her clothes, and then went back to the cottage. She avoided meeting his eyes, not just because she was more than half ashamed of her own response to him, but because she was so afraid he would see in them just how much she needed him.

It was dawning on Rio that male sexuality was a very new phenomenon to her. She'd known that the men who had loved her in the past had never stirred her deeply; but she'd never even remotely guessed just how profound her reactions to a man could be.

The vision of Cameron's naked body was blazing in her mind, seared into her memory like a brand. She had seen male nudity before, but it had been as different from Cameron's as candlelight from the sun. Where the nakedness of other men had been pale, shameful, somehow distasteful, his had been glorious. She would always carry with her that image of velvety, sun-kissed skin, of hard muscle, of the proud virility between his thighs.

Impossible not to wonder how he would look in arousal, what his lovemaking would be like. Yet the thought was shocking, bringing the blood rushing to her face and throat, making the muscles of her womb seem to melt as though his touch were already there, opening her mysteries . . .

'I'm going to see if your Land Rover will start this morning,' he said, lifting up the bonnet and delving into the engine, apparently totally unaware of the turmoil he had left Rio in.

Wandering through the deserted rooms of the cottage, hunting for any further scraps of her work that might be remaining, she tried to get her feelings under control.

It occured to Rio that she'd never needed anyone in her life in quite this way. She was so used to the luxury of self-reliance that discovering her dependence on Cameron was like having the ground cut away from under her. It left her emotionally floundering, mortally afraid of being wounded.

What by? His indifference, perhaps, when he'd tired of her. He hadn't denied, for example, that his interest in her was primarily sexual. By now she knew him well enough to trust that he would never force his will on her.

The trouble was that his demonic charm might do the job better than any force. Plenty of women, as he'd said in the firelight, might be glad of the chance. More than glad. His lovemaking would be unforgettable. If the woman existed who would be able to simply take, as men took, and leave him behind with no regrets, then the rewards might be dizzying.

But to have him plunge into her, as he had just plunged into the sea—and then to watch him walk away for ever . . . that would be unbearable.

The sound of the Land Rover's engine firing up reluctantly, then roaring into life, signalled Cameron's success. She leaned on the window-sill, watching him with troubled grey eyes. To the ordinary woman, all too vulnerable to attachments, all too possessive of a man so beautiful and desirable, what prospect invited? Only pain . . .

Her thoughts churned in irresolute circles.

It was almost noon by the time the coastguard launch arrived in the little bay, and nosed its way towards the sandy beach. The two officers who waded ashore carried a duffel-bag of supplies for them—basic toiletries and first-aid materials, clean towels and clothing, and a dozen pre-packed meals in tin-foil cartons. There would, Rio hoped hungrily, be at least *some* vegetables in all that lot.

'Bloody glad to see you both alive,' was the greeting they got. 'The Cotton Foundation have been in a panic about you, Miss Faber. And the media are all in a fluster. You're probably going to run into reporters at some stage over the next few days.'

'I can wait,' Cameron said ironically.

They also brought sobering news of the outside world.

'Death toll's risen to seven so far,' the senior officer informed them laconically. 'There are probably a damned sight more, mostly fishermen and sailors. If it had gone through Darwin, the way it sometimes does, there would have been ten times that. Usually takes a couple of days to get the whole ungodly mess sorted out.'

The information suddenly put it all in perspective for Rio. She'd been slightly ashamed of their raggedy appearance until now, but suddenly it hardly seemed to matter any more. Seven lives lost in that terrible assault, seven families bereaved and desolated . . . But for Cameron, she herself might have been one of those missing lives.

They showed them Trixie's path on their chart, an erratic zigzag of destruction that had miraculously missed any high concentrations of population. 'She's blowing herself out somewhere in the Coral Sea right now. The islands are getting rough weather, but it probably isn't going to be very serious.'

'Looks like your place missed the worst of it, Mr Frazer.' The coastguard tapped the tiny dot on the map marked Barramundi with his finger. 'It almost always does. They call it luck, but I'd say your great-grandfather knew a thing or two about weather patterns.'

'I'd say so, too,' Cameron smiled. Rio glanced at his bronzed face in puzzlement. Was Cameron a descendant of those old Prior-Jordans? That would explain a lot of things . . .

They walked up the beach together.

'Strewth!' the younger coastguard said, looking at the cottage with wide eyes. 'That's the worst we've seen so far. You must have been slap bang in the path of the cyclone.' He glanced at them with awe. 'How the hell you two managed to survive is beyond me.'

'It took some concentration,' Cameron said drily.

'What are your plans?' the other asked. 'You can't stay here. We're heading back down the coast now, looking for wreckage. We can drop you off at Cooktown if that suits you.'

Cameron shook his dark head. 'We're going the other way, in the vehicles. Miss Faber's going to be staying with me at Barramundi for the next couple of weeks.'

'There's certainly nothing much here to stay for,' the officer nodded. He gave Rio a quick glance, a half-smile, tugging at his lean mouth. 'Ever been to Barramundi, Miss Faber?' She shook her head. 'It's a beautiful place,' he assured her. 'Beautiful. You'll love it.'

'Will I?' She looked away, irritated by that knowing glint in his face. Was that the usual male appraisal in the two officer's eyes? Or was there a lip-smacking appreciation at the thought that she'd soon be in Cameron Frazer's bed? She damned well wouldn't be, she assured herself grimly. So they could put that in their pipes and smoke it.

To Rio's utter disgust, the coastguard's twelve tin-foil cartons had all contained the same rich stew. A meat stew. 'I *asked* them for vegetables,' she wailed. Ignoring Cameron's ironic expression, she refused point-blank to touch any of it.

'We'll leave it for the gulls,' he'd shrugged, deciding not to eat at all if he couldn't eat with her.

The end result was that they set off for Barramundi without a thing to eat.

For her own part, Rio's stomach was clamouring for nourishment as she steered the Land Rover carefully after Cameron's red jeep down the pot-holed and branch-strewn road north. It was by now blisteringly hot, and the wheel burned her hands.

The Land Rover had always been rather too heavy for her to handle with ease. She was hardly in a good mood to start with, and it didn't improve as the heat rapidly dried out the wet earth, so that clouds of yellow dust were beginning to bedevil the road. That choking Australian dust! She knew it so well, from endless journeys in Maudie's ancient Holden.

Now it billowed up from Cameron's wheels, completely obscuring the jeep from her view. It filled the Land Rover, so that she was forced to wind up the window, and suffer the stifling heat.

It hid the worst pot-holes from view, so that she lurched

over them sickeningly, with no time to swerve. She hung back further, but the cloud seemed to wait for her, hanging luminously in the air.

The jolting very soon gave her a filthy headache. A premonition, she decided grimly, of what would be in store for her if she allowed herself to get involved with Cameron Frazer. 'This could be the most stupid move you've ever made,' she muttered to herself through rattling teeth.

After a couple of hours of misery, the track joined a brief stretch of tarred road. Cameron turned down it, and she followed him towards the sea again. In half an hour they had reached a little town, which announced itself, on an appropriately twisted signboard, as Skewes Bank.

It was a tiny, dusty place, with an atmosphere of parched desert remoteness, even though it overlooked the sea. Its slightly battered air might have been due to Cyclone Trixie, but might just as well have been usual at any time of the year. Cameron waved an arm to suggest that they stop here.

Faded-looking Coke and Fanta signs on a whitewashed building in the main street suggested that it might provide refreshments. It wasn't until they'd stopped and got out that they saw the broken-off sign propped next to the doorway, reading *Sea View Diner*. The pavements were also thick with beach-sand and pieces of seaweed. Trixie had obviously passed this way. It was bakingly hot on the street, but the interior was cool and fly-free.

'Fish and chips is all I've got,' the tired-looking woman behind the counter told them flatly. 'We're still waiting for the supply wagon. But the fish is fresh. You want it?'

Rio looked at Cameron, and shrugged tiredly. She was too hungry to object now. Both of them pale ochre with dust, they sat at a window-table in silence, and stared out at the promenade, and the distant, deep blue sea. An open truck had been parked on the pavement, and a team of men were shovelling up the sand to clear the gutters. But hardly anyone else was stirring in the street outside.

'Big blow, night before last,' the tired-looking woman

commented laconically as she brought their food. 'Coffee, too?'

'Please,' Cameron replied.

She nodded, and studied their dusty and ragged appearance incuriously. 'You two get caught in the cyclone?'

'Something like that.'

'You were darned lucky to survive, then.' She nodded again, then went to get the coffee.

'This place gives me *déjà vu*,' Rio smiled at him. 'I ate in so many dumps like this with Maudie. I wonder how many towns like Skewes Bank there are in all of Australia?'

'I'm fond of them too,' he nodded, deep eyes half closed as he leaned back in his chair. 'But they tend to put me to sleep.' He looked weary, but unbelievably handsome. He stretched with a sigh, the muscles tightening across his chest.

As the tired-looking woman had promised, the crisply battered fish and chips were delicious. The meal reminded Rio of countless Oxford evenings during her undergraduate years, and she ate with the relish of a hungry young animal.

'If you're not careful,' Cameron commented, 'you're going to turn back into a carnivore.' She looked up at him guiltily. His dark blue eyes were amused, but not mocking.

'The coastguard said something about Barramundi being built by one of your ancestors,' she said, licking her fingers with a dainty tongue. 'That can't be right, can it?'

Cameron nodded. 'It's right enough.'

Her grey eyes widened. 'Then you're a Prior-Jordan?'

'My mother was.' He half smiled at her wide grey eyes. 'Don't look so impressed. The family may have been fabulously wealthy during the last century, but all those English millions just disappeared into the ground at Laura Bay. There's no fortune left.'

'But the house?' she queried.

'Barramundi belongs to me. It was about the only thing my grandfather had to leave my mother when he died.'

'You sound slightly bitter,' she commented, wondering whether she'd detected a note of resentment in the deep voice.

Cameron shook his head. 'Not any more.'

Rio speared a crisp piece of fish. 'Then you were bitter once. What at—the waste?'

'Partly.'

'But it was a noble venture,' she protested, 'what I know of it, anyway. You can't blame them for trying.'

'I blame them for failing,' he said silkily. 'Absolutely nothing about Laura Bay was right for sugar. Not the soil, not the climate, nothing. It was a doomed venture from the very beginning, doomed by greed, vanity and blindness.' A brief smile crossed his lips. 'Even the name was grandiose— *Laura Bay*. They named it after my great-grandmother, and they envisaged fleets of clippers mooring alongside the warehouses, taking fat bags of Prior-Jordan sugar to every quarter of the globe.' He gave her an ironic shrug. 'It's just a crescent of white beach now, with the coconut palms drooping into the water.'

'Loneliest place on earth,' she said softly, echoing his own words.

'That's right,' he nodded, and drained his coffee-cup.

She studied him speculatively. 'Well, well,' she said. 'How glamorous! I never suspected that I had the last descendant of the Prior-Jordans as my saviour all this time.'

'The Prior-Jordans are irrelevant to me, Rio.' There was a grim cast to his face now. 'I have my own life, and their history is not my history.'

'Now it's me treading on your corns,' she said with a slight smile at his seriousness. 'I didn't mean to speak out of turn. You obviously don't like to talk about them.'

'Barramundi has been useful to me,' he answered her obliquely. 'I don't mind talking about my mother's family. I just don't like being identified with them by people who know very little about me.'

'Sorry for breathing,' Rio said drily, and put her knife and fork down. She hated that calm way he snubbed her.

'I've had enough to eat. Is the coffee worth drinking?'

'Not unless you're dying of thirst,' he said shortly. 'Shall we get back on the road?'

'If you say so.'

At the counter Cameron bought a six-pack of beer, and paid for the meal. Feeling decidedly cool towards him, Rio preceded him outside. The team of men was still shovelling steadily at the heaps of sand, sweat glistening on bare backs.

Cameron glanced at her stiff expression as she hauled herself into the Land Rover's cab. He leaned on the window-sill with a muscular brown forearm, dark blue eyes on a level with hers, despite her height above the road. 'Did I snap at you back there?' he asked.

Rio struggled with a retort. 'Yes,' she said finally, 'as a matter of fact, you did.'

'I thought I must have done.' His dark-stubbled cheeks tightened in a slight smile, eyes reaching right into her soul. 'I'm tired, Rio. And you deserve better.' He touched her cheek gently. 'Sorry.'

She watched him walk to his own jeep, wondering what in God's name that enchanting quality was about him that left her weak-kneed. He could bewitch her at will, make her willing to accept a dozen snubs an hour from him—if only he'd apologise for them with that smile that warmed the whole of her body, that all too brief caress of her face . . .

She slammed the Land Rover into gear, cursing her own susceptibility, and followed him down the dusty street.

As she coped with the pot-holed road towards Barramundi, Rio was dredging up all the facts she could recall about the Prior-Jordans and Laura Bay.

They'd been an aristocratic family, as far as she could remember, who'd taken the unheard-of step of leaving nineteenth-century England for the New World. Their saga had become an integral part of northern Queensland's mythology. Something of the romance and legend surrounding Laura Bay had interwoven itself through the sober pages of history—tales of the great house the Prior-Jordans had built themselves on the wild coast, of their extravagant and beautiful women, of the carriages that had ridden from hundreds of miles around to attend the glittering balls they had held.

It was somehow easy to imagine Cameron in some dazzling *salon*, reclining on a sofa with a cigar, enchanting every woman in the room with that smoky smile and those deep blue eyes. It occurred to her suddenly that he would be absolutely devastating in a formal suit. Any man who could look as good as he did in jeans and a T-shirt would be heart-stopping in silk. A hot glimpse of his nudity crossed her thoughts, and she shook the tanned, sexy image away crossly, concentrating on the Prior-Jordans.

Their great fortune had slowly been dissipated, partly by the slow failure of their sugar empire, and partly through the profligacy of later generations. After a hundred and fifty years, the dark green bush had crept back over the vast fields of sugar-cane they'd planted. The workers had left, the warehouses had fallen into ruin.

She clearly remembered Maudie telling her about the grand old house in the bush, and the way the image had captured her imagination as a girl.

She'd always thought that the Prior-Jordan family had died out, maybe because Maudie had told her so. But obviously Maudie had been wrong. One had been left.

Had Cameron grown up at Barramundi, then? And, if his mother had been a Prior-Jordan as he'd said, who had his father been? And if Barramundi was his own was he funding his own research there?

She'd always simply assumed that, like her, Cameron was working on a grant from some scientific foundation. It was possible, however, that he was paying his own way.

But that would need a vast outlay. She knew from bitter experience that research cost money, and research of the kind she'd been told about in London would cost many thousands; which would suggest that the Prior-Jordan fortune wasn't quite as extinct as the legend had it.

There were suddenly a dozen questions in Rio's mind, teasing her for answers.

But they were answers that would have to wait through this heat, and this swirling yellow dust, until Barramundi.

CHAPTER SIX

'I've just been talking to Brisbane about you.'

Rio half opened her eyes, and raised her face from the pillows, the last vestiges of her dream fading away. Cameron was sitting on her bed, offering her a glass of fruit juice.

She struggled upright, remembering just in time to pull the sheets up over her breasts—she'd fallen into bed naked last night—and took the juice gratefully.

'Brisbane?' she repeated sleepily.

'Your Foundation's Liaison Office,' he nodded. 'They were extremely concerned about you. I said that you were well, and that you'd call them later on this morning.'

'Thanks.' She closed her grey eyes as she took a first sip of the crushed pineapple juice, then pushed her tumbled hair away from her face and smiled at him dreamily. 'So it's all real. I thought it might be a dream.'

'What?'

'All this.' She waved at her surroundings. 'When I was a kid, I used to imagine that heaven would be a little bit like this place.'

'You like it?' he asked, watching her face with warm eyes.

'I love it,' she said simply. She leaned back against the pillows and stared up at the silk canopy above. She was lying in the first four-poster bed she'd ever slept in, surrounded by a room of cool white beauty. 'I've never seen anything like it in my life before.'

'What had you expected of Barramundi?' he asked in amusement.

'Oh . . .' She thought briefly. 'A kind of crumbling subtropical grandeur, I suppose. All cracked plasterwork and overgrown rosebeds—and geckoes on the ceilings.'

'It wasn't too different from that a couple of years ago,' Cameron nodded. 'How do you feel this morning?'

'A bit battered,' she admitted. 'As though I'd run a marathon.' She glanced down at the fine linen that framed her smooth, tanned shoulders. 'And I've probably made these beautiful sheets filthy.'

'You weren't in much of a state to wash last night,' he reminded her gently. 'You must have fallen asleep as soon as your head touched the pillow, like a child. I had to come in and pull the sheets over you, and switch off the lights.' She flushed slightly, as much at the uncomfortable tenderness of the image as at her own naïveté, and Cameron smiled slightly. 'As long as you're all right.'

'Just a bit bruised,' she nodded. 'I'll be ten times better after a shower.'

'Good.' He rose to leave, pausing in the doorway, tall and rangy in denims and a South Sea Island cotton shirt. 'I'm going down to the shark tanks. If you want any more breakfast, it's all laid out in the kitchen.' Blue eyes smiled at her. 'Just take your time.'

She watched him leave, still holding her glass in both hands. In the aftermath of everything that had happened, she was starting to feel that she had known Cameron Frazer all her life. And that was despite the fact that he never stopped surprising, and occasionally infuriating, her.

Waking up to see his tanned face, opening her eyes to meet that deep blue gaze, gave her a weird sense of *déjà vu*, of having been here before.

Except that she'd never been anywhere remotely like Barramundi in her life.

This morning, as she got out of bed and looked around her, she was still trying to come to terms with the wild beauty of the place. The first glimpse she'd had of it, climbing wearily out of the Land Rover yesterday, had made her heart rise in her breast like a bird.

The old colonial mansion, its beauty untouched by the

cyclone which had just passed, had moved her as no house had ever moved her in the past. If she couldn't write a magnificent report in these surroundings, then she couldn't do it anywhere.

A bathroom adjoined her bedroom, all mahogany and painted white porcelain, furnished to a woman's exquisite taste. The shower in it was a very different proposition from the crude affair at the cottage. She arched her youthful body to the torrent that sprayed from the big brass rose, the warm water flowing down the sleek lines of her breasts and flanks.

It was joy to wash her hair, and soap away the salt and dust of yesterday's journey. When she looked in the mirror afterwards, something more like her normal face stared back at her, the soft grey eyes so cool in the honeyed oval of her face, her naturally blonde hair bleached to platinum by her weeks in the sea and the sun.

It had never ocurred to Rio to wonder whether she was beautiful before. It had always seemed to her that she was sufficiently attractive to men not to have to feel insecure. But as she studied her own mouth and eyes in the mirror, she found herself suddenly wishing for true beauty. Beautiful women seemed to lead such fulfilled lives. Every plum fell so naturally into their laps. They had the confidence to deal with a man like Cameron Frazer on his own terms.

But the face which looked seriously back at her from the gilded mirror seemed so defenceless—almost girlish, in fact, with its full mouth and long lashes, with no touch of cosmetic sophistication to add a layer of elegance.

And short of reddening her lips with the red berries of the cotoneaster which grew in the garden, she now had no access to that kind of elegance, because every single item of her sparse toiletries had been lost at the cottage.

Sighing, she padded back into the bedroom, and dressed herself in a clean pair of jeans and a cotton shirt—obviously Cameron's—which she found in the cupboard, and which was deliciously cool on account of being far too big.

It was all too easy to imagine an affair between them when she thought back to the way he'd kissed her. But when she looked around now, thought it all through . . .

That he would want her body was something she could accept. But that he could ever want anything deeper than that was something she now found it almost impossible to believe.

Especially now that she had seen Barramundi, and had begun to realise that Cameron Frazer, far from being an impoverished scientist like herself, was very likely a man of considerable wealth.

Barramundi might have been crumbling once, but it had been restored to a perfection that was quite extraordinary, given the isolation of its setting. And it was big enough to need the staff of at least a dozen people, mostly married Filipino couples, who kept the house and gardens in such immaculate order.

She didn't even have to make her bed; every aspect of her life, from the spotless condition of her clothes to her delicious meals—vegetarian, as Cameron had promised— was taken care of by some gentle, smiling servant. They plainly worshipped Cameron, and that worship extended to her by proxy. In the old colonial style, they lived in bungalows set away from the mansion itself, and it was they who did all the household shopping at the nearest town, Musgrave.

The house itself, Rio was realising, had been built to satisfy two overwhelming imperatives—the requirements of nineteenth-century elegance and the eternal North Australian weather. Verandas ran the full length of the house on both the upper and lower floors, and all the rooms had toweringly high ceilings, allowing the air to circulate.

In the garden, fountains and waterfalls tempted you away from the blazing heat of midday, and benches were set under shady trees, where an *amour*, or a business conversation could be carried on in private. The magnificence of its setting made a perfect foil to the soaring grace of the house.

Barramundi was an exquisite, entirely Australian mansion. There was a multitude of English touches—she had a clear memory from last night of portraits of dark-eyed Prior-Jordans on the high walls, the beautiful furniture in every room, the chandeliers and brocades, the Indian and Chinese screens and vases. But the house remained a masterpeiece of colonial design. She wasn't an expert on architecture, but Barramundi must be one of the most beautiful period houses in Australia.

Which all emphasised her original realisation—that, despite the freedom of Cameron Frazer's life, he was a rich man. Not just in the possession of the house he had inherited; the restoration must have cost a fabulous sum in itself. And here was a mystery, because Cameron had already acknowledged that the Prior-Jordan fortune was long since gone. Where, then, had the money for Barramundi come from?

And if he had spent so much time and wealth restoring the place, what explained his odd ambiguity about it and his ancestors? The way he'd snapped at her in Skewes Bank still rankled. It was hard to work out why he should be so touchy about an inheritance as grand as Barramundi. There was even a stable-block, and he'd told her that six horses were kept there, on the off chance that he or one of his guests might want to ride them . . .

Sighing, Rio pulled her hair away from her face. It was marvellous to feel it clean and silky between her fingers again, to feel her soft skin free of salt and grime. What was the point of speculating about Cameron? She was here to write up her report, not to engage in a love affair with a stranger.

She had to remember that!

Rio walked down through the garden to find him. It was literally a blaze of colour, the tibouchina flowering beside the scarlet trumpets of hibiscus and the icy white bracts of arum lilies, a riot of flowers she couldn't even begin to name. In the midst of it all, a small fountain sprayed glittering diamonds of water into the air, refreshing the heat with moist music.

Beyond the garden, a belt of palm trees sheltered the house from the sea. Its tempting blueness could just be seen over the dark green fronds. She made her way in that direction, enjoying the feel of the sun on her clean skin. After the chaos of the past weeks, this was like a heavenly oasis of calm and beauty.

The garden ended at the first line of palms, beyond which the scientific area clearly began. She'd been expecting something spectacular of Cameron's shark tanks, and she wasn't disappointed.

There were three of them, wide blue discs set in the lee of the palm belt. As she got closer, Rio could see that two of them were at least fifty feet across, the third slightly smaller. Beside them stood a prefab hut, which no doubt housed the electronic equipment Professor Murdoch had told her about in London.

Cameron himself was squatting at the edge of one of the pools, watching the water intently, with a clipboard in the crook of one arm.

Rio joined him at the brink, then stepped back with a gasp. The pool was around ten feet deep. In its clear depths, the torpedo shape of a very big shark cruised with lazy power. She could clearly see the gills rippling on either side of the muscular head, and as it turned with a flick of its tail, she saw the cold black eyes gleam dully.

'God!' She squatted beside him, her arm brushing his. 'How big is he?'

'He's a she,' he smiled briefly. 'Monica's about four years old, and she weighs something like half a ton.'

'*Monica?*'

'I named her after an old friend,' he said expressionlessly, 'of whom she reminds me occasionally.'

'Some friend,' Rio muttered. The huge shark moved with awesome speed, each lazy sweep of its arched tail propelling it forward effortlessly. The rough skin was grey on top, paling to cream under its belly and at the tips of its rigid fins, and as it surged past them Rio saw the sickle-shaped mouth, gaping slightly open.

'Sharks have to keep swimming,' Cameron told her, his eyes following Monica's progress. 'As soon as they stop moving, they sink.'

'How on earth did you get this animal into the tank?' Rio asked in awe.

'She was netted by the Australian Shark Board, not more than fifty miles down the coast. They brought her up here in a specially adapted trawler.'

'Oh.' Rio felt a chilly finger touch the nape of her neck as she watched Monica swim with deadly grace through the sunlit water. She'd known that sharks lived in the water she dived in every day, but it was a different sort of knowledge to see a twelve-foot specimen swimming at her feet.

'Makes you think, doesn't it?' She looked up quickly to see that Cameron had been reading her thoughts, and was smiling at her with a dry quirk of one eyebrow.

'Hmmm,' Rio agreed uncomfortably. 'She's a white-pointer, isn't she?'

'Yes. One of the commonest species in tropical waters, right around the globe. Potentially very dangerous, but not noted as man-killers. Monica is proving very useful for my research.' He rose fluidly, and led her to the next tank. 'These fellows are rather different.'

There were two sharks in the other big tank, each one slightly longer than the white-tipped shark, but paler in colour. Their shape was different, too. They had sleekly muscled bodies with ugly, battered faces, like mindless underwater gangsters. These creatures were fashioned with a deadly purpose that she recognised with an instant chill.

'Great whites,' she said quietly.

Cameron nodded, his eyes following them as they circled the tank in a silent ballet. 'Grade-A specimens,' he said easily. 'They're born with all the instincts they need to be perfect killing machines. Their behaviour never changes, because they don't need to learn anything. Practically everything else in the sea, including man, is just breakfast, lunch, or supper to them. They account for the vast majority of all shark attacks on humans.'

'Do you like them?' she asked curiously, wondering how such a beautiful man could feel an affinity with such sinister creatures.

'Most people who work with sharks come to admire them,' he smiled. 'They're remarkable animals. As for liking them——' He stared broodingly at the two sharks in the tank. 'I think "respect" is a better word than "like". They're too destructive to inspire much affection. These two came from the same source, by the way.'

'Is that who you're working for?' Rio asked him. 'The Shark Board?'

'They will eventually profit from any success I might have,' Cameron nodded. 'But the ASB is only one of the interested parties. Sharks are a major menace for commercial and military divers who have to work in warm seas. They also represent a very real threat to anyone in the water after shipwrecks or airplane crashes. No one has ever devised a really effective way of deterring them.'

'Then who *is* paying for your research?' Rio pressed, looking from the huge tanks to Cameron's face.

'Why should anyone be paying?' He gave her a slight smile. 'I assembled this equipment at my own expense, and the tanks have been here for years. I get help, but it tends to be of a physical nature, rather than financial.'

'It must have cost a fortune. It must be costing you a fortune to keep this whole thing running every day. I don't understand what you're doing it for!'

'I'm doing it in order to try and develop a product which I can market.' He folded muscular arms and looked down at her with amused blue eyes. 'Hadn't that occurred to you?'

'You mean your research is *commercial*? Who do you work for?'

'I have my own company.'

Rio stared at him for a moment, then shook her golden head. 'No, that certainly hadn't occurred to me.'

'Why not?'

'Well, for one thing, commercial research is usually carried out in laboratories, with large staffs of white-coated assistants,' she pointed out. 'It's very unusual for people with their own companies to live like hermits for months at a time, the way you've been doing.'

His smile faded at the perception of her remarks. 'You're probably right,' he said wryly.

Rio turned back to the tank, noting the cables of electronic monitoring equipment that ran into the water. There were glass panels along the side of the tank, under the water level. Behind them, she guessed, would be cameras and microphones, controlled from the prefab hut. A very professional, very expensive set-up. 'What's your company called?' she asked, watching the big sharks glide through the water.

'It's called BTS Ltd,' he said indifferently.

Rio stiffened for a second, her cool grey eyes widening in astonishment. Then a tight smile spread slowly across her mouth.

'I might have known,' she said quietly, almost to herself. 'Biotechnology Systems. I might have known.'

'You've heard of it?' he asked, his expression relaxed, but also watchful.

'There can't be too many biologists who haven't heard of it,' Rio said gently. She looked at Cameron with new understanding, recognising the power and authority that sat so visibly on this man. And she'd once thought he might do well in business—if he tried! 'If it's of any interest to you,' she went on, 'I was going to ask your company for a job when I'd finished my report.'

'There's nothing to stop you from doing so still,' he said calmly.

'Yeah—me and a couple of hundred other unemployed scientists,' she said with a touch of acid in her voice. There simply wasn't a bigger or more prestigious company than Biotechnology Systems. To work for BTS had been the dream of every biology student in her graduation year, but they'd all known that only the cream of them had any chance of fulfilling that dream.

Financially speaking, biology had always been among the least rewarding of the sciences. Biology graduates expected to land jobs with breweries, fertiliser companies, research institutes—places where their skills would be at best selectively used, usually under-used.

BTS was very different. BTS was a living embodiment of a new principle, that biology had vast reserves of untapped potential to affect man's future. The company had produced some of the most brilliant work of the past five years. In the field of power generation from bio-systems, the great research area of the future, BTS was pre-eminent. It also covered half a dozen other fields, from new techniques of crop production to animal genetics.

Why hadn't that old simpleton Professor Murdoch reminded her who he was? More to the point, why hadn't his name rung a loud bell the first moment she'd heard it? She'd never seen a picture of him, but if she'd been asked to name the head of Biotechnology, it would have come to her mind at once ...

She had a sudden vision of Cameron kneeling in the kitchen of her cottage, repairing her fridge.

Of his potent arms shielding her from the cyclone.

Of his naked body so close to hers on the beach.

'I'm sorry,' she said heavily, turning away. 'I've been very, very stupid. But I haven't realised who you were until now.'

'I know that,' he said gently. He moved to her side, but didn't touch her. 'It's been rather pleasant.'

'For you, maybe.' In the silence that followed, Rio thought painfully of her own folly. And she couldn't help feeling an unreasoning anger building up inside her. He'd been watching her make a fool of herself. He'd allowed her to snub him, to cheek him, to treat him with childish carelessness. And all the time, no doubt, he'd been laughing at her näiveté behind that golden façade. Cameron Frazer, head of BTS, foremost of the new breed of technological biologists, flirting with an ignorant young postgraduate who didn't even know who he was . . .

How could she have known, though? It was hardly likely that a man as high-powered as Cameron Frazer would be found living alone on a remote stretch of Australian coastline.

She turned to him, her eyes coolly resentful. 'I still don't understand what you're doing here,' she said tightly. 'You could pay someone to do this research. You surely don't need to hide yourself away out here—isn't your company missing you all this time?'

'I fly to London from time to time,' he replied in the same quiet way. 'Things get along without me perfectly well while I'm on sabbatical.'

'Is that what you call it?' she queried, looking at him from under long lashes.

He ignored her question, replying with one of his own. 'Does the fact that you've realised who I am change anything between us?'

'I don't see how it can't change things,' Rio said shortly.

'That would be a pity.' Unexpectedly, he slid his arm round her waist, and pulled her towards him. She looked up into his dazzling smile, feeling her heart contract at his beauty. 'Forget about BTS,' he said huskily. 'Let's even forget about your report for today. Let Barramundi be that heaven you've always dreamed about, Rio. There's so much time for seriousness, later.' He kissed her mouth gently, his lips warm and commanding. 'Come on,' he ordered, leading her away from the poolside, back towards the house. 'You're due to telephone Brisbane about now. There are people worrying about you in dusty offices. Besides, I've been wanting to show you round the house all morning. Shall we go?'

'The destruction, even the total extinction, of the coral-producing metazoa would probably pass largely unnoticed by the general public.'

Rio paused, staring with unseeing eyes at the typewriter keyboard for a moment. Then she launched back into the final paragraph of her first chapter, neat fingers punching at the keys with precision and force.

'Yet their plight represents a miniature of a much larger picture,' she wrote. 'The world's oceans are being polluted as never before, by the discharge of heavy metals like mercury, by the ever-present and ever-increasing levels of oil—even by the deliberate dumping of lethally toxic materials like nuclear waste and chemical warfare weapons. It is a situation——'

She paused, grimaced, then corrected her last word to 'scandal'.

'It is a scandal which continues despite the glaring fact that in man's immediate future, the oceans are going to have to provide a vastly greater proportion of his food than ever before. The oceans are a source of protein which may represent the only possible solution to the imminent tragedy of a terminally overpopulated and undernourished earth.'

Rio typed up the footnotes, then wound the sheet out of her typewriter. She leaned back in the wicker chair, picking up the glass of pineapple juice, and looked down the long veranda. The high, wide, slatted doors of her bedroom were open, giving her a view of the cool white room within. Against the shady interior, the windows afforded dazzling glimpses of the sunlit, exotic garden outside.

The words she'd just written had come directly from Cameron.

Even some of the phrases were exactly as he'd spoken them, during the many quiet conversations they'd had, sitting close together on the beach, watching the sea together, or wandering in the beautiful garden, hand in hand.

Yet she had no sense of having stolen his ideas. What he'd said had struck so deep a chord with her that it had already become part of her own being. It was as though she'd been waiting all her life for Cameron Frazer. Waiting for his intelligence and breadth of vision to give words to her innermost feelings.

In the week since she'd learned that he was the head of Biotechnology, Rio had come to understand a great deal more about the man who had saved her life during the cyclone. With a kindness that she'd never experienced before, Cameron had been showing her the wonders of Barramundi, as if he had nothing better to do with his time than amuse her, his personal castaway.

Her respect for him had deepened dramatically. Prejudice and silly resentment had coloured her initial attitude towards him. Now, Rio was beginning to understand just how special a man she had been dealing with for so long.

As if by mutual consent, that intense sexual attraction between them had remained undeveloped, neither of them referring to it by any word or action.

It was almost as though, now that his true identity had been unmasked, Cameron's delicious flirtation with her had ended. Had it all, then, been a game to him? A game that had only been possible because she hadn't realised he was a man who'd had a massive success in her own field, and who was probably a multi-millionaire? And, if so, how far would he have gone before the game ended?

Uneasy questions. Irrelevant ones, because in the past week their relationship had deepened into a friendship that went way beyond the physical. She'd learned that behind those intensely blue eyes, Cameron Frazer carried an intellect of great power and sensitivity, a nature that was as warm and strong as the Coral Sea itself.

He was, she thought wryly, the complete Renaissance man. Physically magnificent, endowed with a towering intellect, witty, charming, sexy ... a man whom she was beginning to find devastatingly attractive.

Rio Faber had always felt a contempt for purely physical attraction. The emptiness of most sexual relationships had made them seem worthless to her. What she was starting to feel for Cameron was very different, though. If she'd been sixteen, it could have been called a schoolgirl crush.

Hero-worship.

That obsession with a man which made you love everything he did, everything he said, which made you dream of him at night and moon over him by day. The sort of obsession that made you repeat his ideas, that made you desire him with an ache that intensified every day, every hour, every minute.

Except that she wasn't sixteen. She was a very mature twenty-two, a woman who'd known man's love before, and who ought to have known perfectly well what she was doing.

What would you call it, then? When she thought about it, Rio had to acknowledge that she'd stopped believing in love a long time ago. She'd learned that love was an illusion. At best, it was a pretty name to cover the first excitement of animal lust. At worst, it was a self-delusion which could lead grown men and women into the most absurd and ridiculous behaviour they were capable of.

What, then?

She did not know. All she knew was that she didn't want this time to end.

She wanted to stay here with Cameron, at Barramundi, for ever. She wanted to lose herself in the warm depths of his personality, letting him soak into every fibre of her being.

Rio had never known such an absence of loneliness before. It was a miraculous gift, which he alone had been able to give to her. No man had possessed it before: no, not even Maudie had possessed it. And yet he gave it so freely, the gift of his company. When Cameron was with her it was as though she'd never known what it was like to be without him. Her soul was filled with his presence, and she had no ambition beyond listening to him, watching him, loving him, for the rest of her life.

Which was why a whole week had slipped by before she'd even started getting down to her report. With any sense of urgency removed, now that she had a more or less unlimited stay of leave at Barramundi, it had been all too easy to let it slip.

She'd started work on her report for the first time this morning, reckoning that a week's truancy was already far too long—and had been rewarded by a rush of inspiration which must have had something to do with her surroundings.

She got up from her chair, and walked to the edge of the veranda. Down below, a Filipino gardener was skilfully tying back the arching branches of some fragrant flowering creeper.

A province of heaven. Barramundi was indeed a province of heaven. Yet Cameron's world extended away beyond this belt of rustling palm trees, far to the north, where a financial empire waited for his return.

She still had no idea why he had chosen to exile himself at Barramundi for so many months. It was something he never spoke about, and yet, as she grew closer to him, her intuition made Rio certain that some hurt lay buried behind his decision to withdraw from public life for so long.

At first, she'd jealously wondered whether an unhappy love affair might have driven him away from London. But that was too facile an answer. Cameron wasn't the sort of man to let his equilibrium be destroyed by any woman.

The best answer she could come up with was that some personal crisis had taken place in his life, making him need the space and solitude of Barramundi.

Yet, with her arrival here, that space and solitude had been significantly reduced. Did he resent her presence at Barramundi? She prayed not, and indeed there seemed no sign of it.

And she almost shied away from finding out any more. She didn't want to know any reason that might one day tear him away from her. There were so many things in his life that would eventually separate him from her. BTS, his friends, the women he had left behind him—all the trappings of the life that he had abandoned, yet which she knew with utter certainty he would one day, maybe soon, want to take up again ...

A life that was uniquely filled with success and achievement. What place in it could she possibly hope to occupy? Against the vastness of Cameron Frazer's interests and achievements, her own love for him seemed to dwindle to the insignificance of sparrow's tears. She had taken much from him. Did she really have anything to give in return?

It ocurred to her with a sharp prickle of tears that she'd never had anything to give anyone ...

The beautiful garden blurred in her sight, a hard lump filling her throat with grief at her own helplessness to make Cameron care for her.

'Dreaming?'

She swung round at the sound of Cameron's voice, then turned back to the garden, too late to hide the tears that glistened in her misty grey eyes.

'Just taking a break,' she said, trying to sound normal.

'You're crying,' he said quietly. The touch of his arms encircling her made her shudder with release. She closed her eyes, spilling the salt tears that had gathered on her lids, and pearls splashed warmly on his tanned skin.

'Rio,' he murmured, his mouth close to her ear, and drew her close against him, the power of his arms infinitely comforting around her. 'What is it, little one?'

'It's nothing. Foolishness.' She rested her cool cheek against his shoulder, trying to get her unsteady breathing under control. He stroked her silky hair with tenderness, waiting for her to speak. Her heart yearned to him with a passion that made her think it would surely break ...

He kissed her wet lashes, the salt of her tears bringing a compassionate smile to the curve of his mouth. 'Life's too short for tears. Tell me what it is.'

But she couldn't tell him the reason for her tears, and with an effort she pulled away from his strength and warmth, afraid that she would betray herself by some incautious word.

'I've got to the end of my first chapter,' she told him,

leaning back against the railing, and smiling at him with moist eyes.

'Already?' He walked over to her typewriter, and studied her last page briefly. 'At this rate your stay here is going to be a brief one,' he mused.

'Oh, the first couple of chapters are easy to remember. The later ones are going to take a lot more time.' Rio's eyes met his quickly, then she looked down at her own bare feet, embarrassed by the implication that she was in no hurry to leave Barramundi. 'You'll probably get sick of the very sight of me.'

'I don't think so,' he said gently. He moved over to her, and leaned beside her. She could smell his skin, clean and fresh from the swim he'd taken that morning. 'But Barramundi is a very lonely place for a young girl, Rio.'

'You always say that.' She looked up at him. 'I don't get any impression of loneliness here, Cameron.'

He smiled slightly. 'Apart from the servants, there isn't a soul for miles in any direction.'

'There's you.' The words seemed to express so much more than she meant them to that she flushed slightly, and turned away. 'It's just so perfect here. I've never seen such a beautiful place. I think I could live here for ever.'

'I thought you were so bewitched by the outdoor life?' he teased. 'I seem to remember you once bemoaning the fact that you were caught between four walls.'

'This is different. To live in a place like this isn't remotely like living in a house in some city. This is freedom.' She glanced up at the airy roof, smiling dreamily. Even now, so many features of the house charmed her. The way the immense doors and windows had been made as if for giants, not only for ventilation, but to emphasise that fantastic air of grandeur. The way the garden had been planted so as to make each view a delight. The polished yellow-wood floors throughout. Her bed, a four-poster of such toweringly high coolness that she felt as though she were sleeping under the palanquin of some Oriental despot. 'I was just thinking how very, very beautiful you've made Barramundi.'

'Is that why you were crying when I came in?' he asked mildly.

'Oh, forget that,' she said with a self-conscious laugh.

'I don't like to see tears in your eyes,' he said gently. 'You don't strike me as a woman who would cry for no reason.'

'Women cry for all sorts of reasons,' she said, pulling her white-gold hair back into a ponytail, and securing it with a rubber band. The movement showed off the slim elegance of her tanned arms, emphasising her long, slender neck, and bringing the peaks of her breasts into relief against the blue silk blouse she was wearing.

Cameron's eyes seemed to glint as he studied her body for a moment, then she realised it was just a reflection of the sun.

'So what's your reason for crying?' he asked.

'Nothing in particular,' she assured him. 'There really isn't a reason at all.'

His eyes were watchful. 'You're not unhappy—or lonely?'

'No.' She shook her head, her voice soft. 'That isn't the reason.'

'Good.' He'd obviously resolved not to probe her any further. 'Ever done any sailing?' he asked her.

'Not for years.'

'There's a yacht in the boathouse,' he said, watching her expression brighten with excitement. 'I reckon you've earned some recreation. Shall we take it out this afternoon?'

'I'd love to,' she said breathlessly, grey eyes taking on a joyous blue that seemed to reflect his own gaze.

'Good! I'll ask Joseph to break out the sails.' He held out his hand with a smile. 'In the meantime, make me a promise—no more tears. Right?'

'Right,' she nodded.

'That's settled, then. How about lunch?'

CHAPTER SEVEN

SUNLIGHT flooded the days that followed.

For almost the first time in her life, there were no more questions in Rio's life. Her happiness was total, a mingling of excitement and swelling passion that seemed to be opening in her like a magic flower.

She barely had time to work on her report, yet the delay had long since ceased to bother her. Nothing mattered any more, nothing except Cameron.

He was showing her a world which she'd scarcely dreamed could exist. So many sensations that she would never forget. The surging deck of a yacht under her bare feet, the tautness of sails and lines under her learning fingers. The feel of a horse between her thighs, the wind streaming through her hair as Cameron urged her to gallop across the rough meadows to the north of Barramundi. The bliss of just basking in the sun beside him, talking in the intimate, soft way they'd evolved.

Already, they talked in a shorthand that seemed to bypass ordinary modes of conversation. He seemed to know what she meant to say even before she'd formed the words on her tongue; and there was so much that no longer needed saying between them at all.

Yet she never approached boredom with him—not even familiarity, indeed—and she prayed that he felt the same about her.

Their quarrel over her vegetarianism was still sputtering on; he mocked her for what he called her 'selective conscience', she him for his bloodthirstiness. There was no malice in either taunt. It was the kind of antagonism that made their tenderness all the more sweet.

Rio could never get over her initial respect for the power of his mind; instead, her awe of him simply kept growing,

104

as she learned just how much there was to him, what depths
and heights his spirit contained.

Nor could she ever control her reaction to his physical
beauty. The electric shock of his muscled torso on her senses,
the slamming impact of that deep, hot gaze, the way her skin
prickled up helplessly at his slightest touch—these were
things over which she had as little control as the beating of
her own heart, or the quickening breath in her lungs.

Cameron had unlocked something in her heart, something that had been there since her birth, yet which had
never before been freed. And its freedom had brought a
new phase of existence for her.

Its effect on her was more than emotional. Rio was
changing physically, in subtle but noticeable ways.

The lingering hunger of her tomboy adolescence had
started to disappear from her face and body. Angular
corners were smoothing into lines of pure female elegance;
the girlishly lean shape of her breasts and hips filled out in a
way that was almost—but not quite—imperceptible.

It was as though a long-delayed womanhood was
dawning on Rio Faber, at the age of twenty-two. A
womanhood that filtered into her cheeks and eyes and
mouth, warming her blood, and giving her a mysterious
allure that had only been hinted at before.

There seemed to be a moment, a perceptible instant,
when she trembled on the brink of true beauty; and then,
suddenly, with the magic of the first day of spring, it was
there—the full beauty of Rio's womanhood.

If Cameron noticed these changes in her, and recognised
what had wrought them, he kept that knowledge to himself.

And Rio herself only half understood them. There was a
black and pink bikini in her cupboard at Barramundi.
Whose it was she had never enquired, though the Dior label
spoke of expensive feminine taste, and she'd appropriated it
on her arrival. At first it had fitted her perfectly; but as the
golden weeks passed, she couldn't help noticing that its

covering was no longer quite so adequate. Her breasts had tautened the nylon with erotic fullness, and even the bottom seemed to be clinging more tightly than before.

Her natural conclusion, that she was putting on weight, was denied by the scales in her bathroom. Something else was happening, some blossoming process that didn't involve adopting any superfluous flesh. The same blossoming that curved her mouth, deepened the grey of her eyes, carved the lines of her cheeks and throat into exquisite ripeness.

It was a ripeness that had but one function. And it occurred to Rio to wonder how long she could keep fooling herself that that function didn't exist; because she could no more deny the existence of love than she could deny the existence of Cameron Frazer himself.

Nor had she ever told so many secrets in her life before; Cameron never seemed to tire of listening to her voice, of absorbing her pains and pleasures, the sorrows and joys of her memory. Her experience seemed to be extending to him, as though it was not enough for them that they shared each other's present; with a strange urgency, they needed to share one another's pasts.

Dark or bright, it was all one. Sailing in the sweep of Laura Bay, or riding side by side along the sand, letting the horses find their own pace along the sea's edge, Rio would find herself telling Cameron things that had been forgotten for years, things she'd never believed she could ever share with anyone.

She sometimes wondered whether she'd have found it all so wonderfully new if she'd grown up with brothers and sisters. Yet she suspected that it would have been just as new. Her feelings towards Cameron were not in the slightest degree sisterly. They were something else entirely.

But her deep-rooted fear that Cameron's feelings could never be as deep as hers refused to go away. It was always there, just beneath the surface of her security, waiting to be activated by a chance word or gesture.

On one particularly magnificent afternoon, they took the horses out in a direction they'd not used before, towards the rolling hills above and behind Barramundi.

It was scorchingly hot, and Rio was glad of the wide-brimmed hat Cameron had given her. As they climbed upwards through the sea of golden grass, the perspiration varnished her tanned forearms, and her blouse began to stick to her skin. Moist with the heat, the thin material clung to her perfect breasts so revealingly that the dark aureoles of her nipples were clearly visible through it.

The way Cameron's amused, appreciative blue eyes drifted across her figure told her uncompromisingly that he wasn't oblivious to her femininity, and she kept plucking awkwardly at her blouse to loosen its amorous clinging.

The consolation for the long climb was the gentle breeze that played along the top of the hill, rippling the heads of the grass, and drying their skin with cool relief. The air was slightly less balmy up here, refreshing and clear in her lungs, and the vantage point gave them an excellent view.

They were looking down on Barramundi, the distant red-tiled roof glowing against the greenery of its surroundings, the sea beyond deepening from turquoise in the shallows to the deep ultramarine of further depths.

'What's this place called?' she asked, panting.

'Grey Mare Hill,' he told her, looking down at the scene below them with brooding eyes.

'Are we still on the estate?'

He nodded. 'The estate stretches practically to the horizon.' He urged his horse round to resume the climb. She followed him, recognising with sudden knowledge that these hills must have once borne the fields of sugar-cane for which Barramundi had originally been built.

Yes. It was clear now; she could even detect the traces of ancient cane-breaks in the grass, and here and there the green spike of a surviving sugar-cane plant, naturalised among the lighter vegetation.

As if to confirm her realisation, Cameron reached down, and cut a foot-long stem for her. She studied it as they rode along. It was jointed like a bamboo, but thicker and juicier, and as she cautiously chewed the fibrous stuff, the clear taste of sugar-water flooded her mouth.

A taste of sweetness, she thought that had lured a great English family to these remote hills.

A little further on, they came across what was evidently the ruins of a shed. A derelict horse-buggy stood mournfully outside it, and Rio saw several hoes and other implements lying abandoned among the weeds, with rotting handles and rusty blades.

'Where are we heading?' she asked Cameron.

He nodded at the summit of the hill. 'Up there.'

She followed his gaze. Against the sky, she noticed for the first time that a small church, almost a chapel, was standing among the rippling sea of grass. She could see the iron railings silhouetted against the blue. Beside it stood a curious stone structure with a dome and four miniature turrets, evidently some kind of mausoleum.

She glanced at Cameron's face for an explanation, but he was already leading the way upwards, and she followed him without speaking.

It was a climb of only a few minutes, and then they were dismounting by the weathered iron railings. The sweating horses gratefully lowered their heads to the rich grass.

'What a strange place,' she breathed.

The little chapel had the haunting spell only deserted churches can exert—an atmosphere of the past. A bell still hung in the low tower, and as they stood in silence the wind swayed it slightly, and it clanged with a lonely note in the silence.

The sea of golden grass all around had invaded the churchyard. It was waist-high around the two dozen or so gravestones, giving the place a wild air of solitude and peace.

The gate squeaked rustily as Rio pushed it open, and walked slowly into the churchyard. Though the ornately carved gravestones were now lichen-covered, the legends on them were clearly decipherable. Almost all bore the name Prior-Jordan. Many of the women had the names Alison or Caroline, Geoffreys and Georges predominating among the men. Some of them were children's graves, and some of the dates went back to the beginning of the last century. She turned to look at Cameron, who had been watching her with inscrutable eyes.

'This was the family chapel?' she guessed, and he nodded. 'This was where they worshipped every Sunday,' she mused, half to herself. 'They would come up from Barramundi in a carriage, with all the servants, and enjoy the cool breezes up here. This is where they were baptised and married.'

'And buried,' he added quietly. 'They're all buried here. From first to last.'

'You ought to keep the grass cut,' Rio reproved him, looking around the wilderness.

'I like it better this way.' Cameron smiled.

Rio pushed through the rustling grass towards the stone monument. It was definitely a mausoleum, the entablature beautifully carved with a Grecian frieze. The inscription announced that here lay buried Sir George Prior-Jordan, and his wife, Lady Laura, the original founders of Barramundi. Behind it was a group of smaller graves, obviously belonging to workers on the estate.

'Is your mother buried here, too?' Rio asked him tentatively, broaching a subject which, for all their close intimacy, she had never trespassed on before now.

He nodded, and led her to one of the newer stones. The name upon it was Caroline Frazer, and the date of her death was almost twenty years old. 'How old were you when she died?' Rio asked softly.

'Fourteen,' he replied.

She thought of the London cemetery where her own
parents lay buried. 'And your father?' she ventured.

'He's buried in Scotland,' Cameron told her. 'He died
eighteen months after her.' He took her arm, and walked
with her into the porch of the church.

The door was unlocked, and the interior smelled clean
and dry. There were recent flowers on the altar, and on the
pulpit, and Rio stared at them.

'Joseph and his wife keep the place respectable,' he
explained. His deep voice echoed back from the
whitewashed walls. 'They're very religious.'

'Aren't you?' she asked him.

'I'm a biologist,' he said, stroking her cheek with his
finger, and looking into her eyes with an expression that
made her heart flip over inside her. 'I'm not supposed to
believe in non-material things.'

She smiled, and stared round at the pretty interior,
seeing in her mind's eye the scrubbed Victorian faces, the
cravats and crinolines, almost hearing the shuffle of boots
and the faint wail of a baby. 'It's beautiful here,' she said in
a low voice. 'But very sad.'

'Yes,' he said quietly. He drew her down to sit beside him
on one of the mahogany pews. 'I used to come here as a boy,
Rio, and wander among the tombstones, just as you've been
doing. I, too, used to feel that sadness and beauty
overwhelm me.'

She looked at him. 'Were you born at Barramundi,
then?'

'Yes.' He gave her a dry look. 'I was born into a very *fin-
de-siècle* atmosphere—all potted palms and stuffed lyre-
birds in glass cases. Barramundi was in the last days of its
glory then—which is to say the old place was practically
derelict. My mother and I lived in two of the only three

habitable rooms in the whole house, and my grandparents lived in the other.'

'You must have had a lonely childhood,' she said, looking up into his magnificent face with serious grey eyes.

'Yes,' he nodded. 'A strange, lonely childhood—and even lonelier after my father left for Scotland. My mother had a fierce loyalty to the estate, you see—something my grandparents had drummed into her. She could never have left Barramundi. My mother was beautiful and intelligent, but she was a Prior-Jordan through and through—with all the family's blind pride and folly.' His expression was midway between tenderness and scorn. 'She and my grandparents used to sit in the mouldering old *salon*, and discuss how they were going to rebuild Barramundi, and make Australia ring with the name of Prior-Jordan again. My father eventually decided he couldn't stand it. He went back to Edinburgh, where he'd been born, to find his fortune, and left us here.' Cameron stared around him with dark eyes. 'I used to sit in these pews and swear I'd follow him one day. I'd make my fortune and then I'd come back here and burn it to the ground.'

'But you came back and rebuilt it instead,' she said with a slight smile.

'It was the next best thing,' he grinned. His smile faded as he went on, 'During my childhood, Barramundi wasn't remotely like it is today. It was a lot more like the picture you saw it in your imagination, little one, before you came here. Crumbling and eerie, and filled with geckoes, and very depressing.'

'Not romantic?'

'Romantic? Maybe—in a gloomy way. I was an imaginative child, though, and I grew to destest the old place. You have to understand how Barramundi seemed to a little boy.' She watched him reach after the words, blue eyes half closed. 'It was like an albatross round my neck. A vast failure that seemed to daunt my whole future. My grandparents tried to fill my head with a sense of its past glories, the way they'd done with my mother. But all I could see was something I had to escape from.' He stared at the altar, the stained-glass window reflecting kaleidoscope patterns in his eyes. 'They lived in the past. I can't explain it. They had a kind of blindness to reality. They were charming, cultured people, and they loved me very dearly. But they just couldn't accept that the dream was over.' He grimaced. 'Listening to them, you could see how Barramundi had failed, how a huge fortune had been squandered.'

Rio listened in fascinated silence, trying to see him as the boy he had been, and finding it very hard.

'It seemed to me that there was nothing here but loneliness and decay,' he went on. 'A deserted mansion in a wild and overgrown garden. An empty bay, a lonely beach. Forgotten fields abandoned by their workers. A redundant church up on the hill, and forgotten gravestones among the whispering grass.'

Rio shuddered suddenly, as though something of his emotion had entered her own soul for a moment. 'I hadn't thought of it quite like that.'

'I could think of nothing else.' He took her slender fingers in his hand, and caressed the fine skin, raising the goose-flesh all along her arms. 'I resolved early to escape from it.'

'Leaving your family behind?' she questioned.

'If it had been necessary,' he nodded, 'I would have done. In the end, it didn't come to that. My mother's health had never been good. She died young, and my grandparents didn't survive her for long; and then I was alone at Barramundi, with only a servant or two to keep me company, and the old lawyer telling me there were more debts than assets to the family name.'

His passionate mouth turned down in a half-bitter, half-amused smile. 'At which point,' he said drily, 'the dynasty of the Prior-Jordans had ended for good.'

Cameron rose, and walked slowly up the aisle towards the altar. He leaned on the sandstone slab, absently fingering the bright blooms of the zinnias Joseph's wife had placed there, obviously lost in his memories.

Rio studied his tall figure, wondering how such a strong, almost formidable man could yet be so sensitive.

She sat in silence, his words echoing through her mind. Now, she felt she knew a great deal more about Cameron. He had just given her a profound insight into the reasons for his ambiguous feelings towards Barramundi, his anger at being identified with the Prior-Jordans.

But more, he had shown her something of the mainspring of his very being—the driving need in him to scale the heights, to conquer and achieve. Cameron Frazer, she guessed, needed success more than most men did. It had always represented escape from him, escape from the shadow of Barramundi . . .

'What did you do after they all died?' she asked in a hushed voice.

He turned to look at her, his eyes brightening as though suddenly glad she was there to take him out of his reverie. 'I shut the place up,' he said with a smile, 'and scraped together enough money to join my father in Edinburgh. He was an engineer, a brilliant man in his own way.' He shrugged. 'But unfortunately our reunion was brief. No more than a year. He was killed in an accident at the factory where he worked, and for the second time in my life I found myself alone.'

He pulled a yellow zinnia from the bowl, and walked down the aisle to her, dropping the flower in her lap. Rio reached for his hand, her fingers closing around his in a gesture of sympathy that needed no words. She knew exactly what he had suffered, for she herself had been through those same dark halls.

A glance into her grey eyes was enough to tell him all the things she had no voice to say, and he smiled slightly, leaning down, and kissed Rio on her lips.

It was the first time he had kissed her mouth since the day they had left the wrecked cottage. They had held hands in the intervening weeks, even embraced, but that had been different.

Now, as their lips touched, the full erotic passion that had lain fallow between them all this time suddenly came alive. Rio felt it like a galvanic shock through her system, squeezing her heart and contracting the muscles of her stomach.

She stared into his face, her lips half parted, aware only of her aching need for him. A need that was no longer simply physical, but which had been made a thousand times more intense by all that had passed between them in these golden weeks.

As he continued speaking, she felt her heart pounding in her breast, could feel the blood surging along her veins.

Suddenly her palm was moist against his, and the caress of his fingers was as sexually tormenting as though he were caressing the most intimate secrets of her body.

God! Didn't he know how she felt about him? Surely he could hear her heart beating in the stillness of this empty church? It took a supreme effort for Rio to fight down her emotions, and listen to his calm, deep voice.

She focused herself on his words, trying desperately to ignore the tension in the peaks of her breasts, the hunger in her loins, and follow his description of how he'd completed his schooling in Scotland, had gone to London to study biology at university. This was important, and she didn't want passion to obscure her understanding of it.

'Why biology?' she asked, trying to sound normal, though her lips were dry, and her throat tight with tension. 'Why not economics or business?'

'Because, like you,' he smiled, 'I loved the natural world. I wanted to know more about it. I wanted to understand its workings from a scientific point of view.' He met her eyes.

'You know me well enough by now to know that ecology happens to be one of my passions.'

She nodded. 'But it must have taken a lot of insight to foresee that it would also make you the fortune you needed.'

He shrugged. 'I had no doubt that I would make money, whatever I did; I just wanted to make it in a field that really interested me. Does that sound impossibly vain?'

'It sounds like you,' she answered his smile. 'And Biotechnology Systems? How did that start?'

'Bit by bit,' he shrugged. 'A few moments of inspiration, and a hell of a lot of perspiration. You don't want to hear the whole story.'

'Yes, I do,' said Rio fiercely. 'I want to hear it all!'

Amused by her whimsicality, he sat next to her again, and started talking. It was rare for him to talk about himself for such a length of time, and Rio listened in total fascination as he described the struggle he'd had to convince sponsors and backers that his revolutionary ideas had any foundation. He'd needed so much dedication, so much energy, way beyond what the ordinary man could give.

Yet, knowing him as she did, Rio found a kind of inevitability in it all. He had been born to succeed, and nobody with any understanding of human nature could ever have failed to see that. When he told her casually that he had been a millionaire by the age of thirty, Rio just smiled gently.

He was only in his early prime now, she thought. In a man like Cameron Frazer, that prime would extend well into his sixties, an outpouring of virile energy that would take him—who knew how far, in three decades?

To the heights of not one, but many careers. Anything was open to him—honours, wealth, power, any garland he chose was his for the reaching out and taking.

Once again it came over her, that sense of wonder at his isolation here at Barramundi. Did Cameron Frazer really

have nothing better to do with his time than watch killer
sharks drifting lazily round his private pools—and amuse a
stranger called Rio Faber?

Yet she hated to think of it like that. She needed him so
much. Her stay at Barramundi was becoming increasingly
wondrous to her. It was all too easy to fall into the trap of
thinking that this was for ever.

All too easy to give way to the intoxicating fantasy that
there were no other women in Cameron's life. That she was
his only companion. His lover.

His . . . wife.

The realisation went through Rio with a tingling shock
of self-knowledge. She stared at the altar with cloudy,
unseeing eyes. It was impossible to imagine herself standing
there in a white dress, a demure veil over her face, and a
posy in her hands. Untamed Rio, who had dived naked
in the Coral Sea—was she really longing for the servitude
of marriage? Yet marriage to a man like Cameron
would never be servitude. It would be something far, far
bigger . . .

'So you came back and restored Barramundi,' she said,
wanting to break away from her own dangerous thoughts.
'That must have been a strange experience.'

'It was,' he agreed wryly. 'For a while I toyed with the
idea of selling it. Then, one day, I came up here again and
looked at all those tombstones, and realised that I could
never sell it.' He pulled a bitter-sweet face. 'When your
family insist on having themselves buried in one place, for a
hundred and fifty years, it makes it very hard for
succeeding generations to sell it.'

'But it isn't your home,' she said gently.

'My first home is in London. Barramundi will always be
my second home.'

'An expensive second home,' she smiled, thinking of the
staff he maintained here.

'I'm rich enough not to have to worry about the expense,

Rio. And I come here often for breaks, several times a year.'

'This break has lasted almost five months,' she pointed out, glancing at him. The remark didn't seem to please him very much; he didn't reply to it, in any case, and she sat in silence for a long while, just staring ahead of her, wondering . . .

'I've made you sad,' he smiled at last, reaching out to touch her silky hair.

'No,' she said, drifting out of it, and giving him a quick glance. The last thing she wanted right now was for him to do his mind-reading act with her very intimate thoughts.

'Then I've bored you stiff!' he laughed. 'You've gone all glazed. Let's get back to the house.'

They left the church, and waded through the waist-high grass to where the horses were tethered.

Rio looked back at the little church, her expression wistful. 'Such a lovely, sad place,' she mused. The wind fluttered in her hair, chasing platinum glints off it, the deep blue of the summer sky casting a deeper shadow in her grey eyes.

She stared at the grey stones, thinking how alike she and Cameron were. Both orphaned, both motivated by a deep love of nature. Her lips parted as she sighed gently.

Cameron's gaze was not on the church, but on her face. 'You're so beautiful,' he said softly. 'You have the face of an angel, Rio.'

Flustered, she tried to smile it off, but he was intent, and there was no humour in his expression. Their eyes met, and Rio felt the physical shock of their mutual recognition— recognition of the hunger each felt for the other.

Cameron reached out to her and drew her against the teak-hard strength of his body, his muscles hard yet controlled, as though he was taking a wild bird that might easily be crushed.

'I've ached to hold you like this,' he said in a husky voice, his eyes drinking in the clear, cool grey-green depths of her eyes, the wild-honey glow of her skin. 'If you weren't my guest here, I'd . . .'

'What?' she asked in a voice that was no more than a shaky whisper. But she didn't need to be told what was in his mind. Her lips parted tremulously as she saw the controlled desire in his slow smile.

He kissed her gently, his lips firm and sun-warmed against her own, and her knees were suddenly turning to water. With no volition on her own part, her lips began to open under his, the moistness of her inner mouth yielding to him.

The wind that sighed through the long grass caressed them as they stood locked together by the railings. The horses paused in their browsing to stare at them with soft eyes, then lowered their gentle heads to the grass again.

'Cameron,' she whispered, 'you make me dizzy. I don't think this is very sensible . . .'

His mouth silenced her trite protest with an authority which obliterated every thought in her mind. Warm, velvety, commanding, his lips roamed across her face, hungrily drinking in the scent of her skin, closing hard on the soft petals of her mouth.

Any pretences she'd made at self-control melted now, her yearning rising to meet his as she surrendered the sweetness of her mouth to Cameron, matching the generosity of his passion with a response that was no less ardent.

Their kiss was a journey from the outer appearance of things to their inner reality, from the first brush of lips to the intimate adoration of tongues and clean, hard teeth, until it seemed to her dizzy soul that his mouth was caressing something deep inside her.

'My Rio,' he whispered, drawing back a little in his fierce assault. 'I'm hurting you.'

She looked up at him shakily, her lips feeling bruised. 'You're so strong,' she said unsteadily.

'I'm sorry,' he half smiled, his eyes as deep blue as the sea.

'I wasn't complaining.' She slid her hands across his chest, her fingers spreading across the hard muscles beneath the silk, feeling the pounding of his heart. 'Your strength is wonderful, Cameron. Maybe it's because I have so little myself that I love it so . . .'

'You?' One dark eye brow arched in irony. 'So little strength?'

'Compared to you, yes! You could crush me,' she smiled, with something in her expression that made his eyes glitter.

'You almost make that sound like an invitation,' he growled.

'Perhaps it is,' she said softly.

'I could never crush your spirit. No man could.' He pulled her down on to the soft bank of grass, and laid her on her back, so that she was staring up at him. He leaned over her with a lover's possessive domination, the sun gilding the midnight-dark curls of his hair. 'You're so delicate,' he whispered, 'and yet you're as supple as a willow. No,' he corrected himself with a smile, 'more like something from the sea. A dolphin, maybe.'

'A dolphin!' Rio smiled. 'I'm not sure whether I should be flattered or not!'

He kissed her again, with an erotic expertise that made her gasp out loud. Her slender hands reached beneath his shirt to lay claim to the naked power of his back, revelling in the smooth warmth of his skin. In this moment he was hers, hers utterly, and no one could take him from her.

His mouth was mobile, fiercely desirous, yet never pausing long enough to allow her the satisfaction she ached for. As though deliberately avoiding the soft lips that parted for him, Cameron was kissing her eyelids, the satin skin of her eyelids and temples, the fine curls of platinum hair beside her ears, worshipping her beauty with agonising slowness.

The smell of the crushed grass was sweet all around her, mingling with the smell of his skin and hair. Rio had ached for this for so long that now his passion went to her brain like wine, filling her senses.

Her hands caressed his powerful body, revelling in the ripple of muscles under his smooth skin as he moved against her. Her movements were no longer conscious; her body was responding with a languid surge that expressed all her longing, her sweet undeniable hunger.

'Cameron,' she breathed, her mouth close to the brown column of his throat, 'do you want me as much as I want you?'

'I've wanted you from the moment I saw you,' he whispered. 'You're so lovely, my magical Rio. When I saw you walk up that beach, naked like Aphrodite, I thought I must have spent too long in the sun. You were like a vision of perfection, exquisite and tantalising . . .'

She moaned softly, her eyes fluttering closed as he unfastened the buttons of her blouse, drawing the light cotton away from her gilded shoulders, his rough intake of breath registering the way her naked breasts had affected him. He bent to kiss the exquisite line of her collarbone tasting the trace of salt on the first swell of her breasts.

His lips were warm against her cool skin, the silky caress of his mouth an adoration. She ached fiercely to feel the hunger of his mouth on her nipples, yet he was so slow, teasing her unbearably . . .

How childish she had thought other men, when they had hungered for her breasts, like babies! For the first time, she understood just how much that age-old kiss could express between a man and a woman; she felt herself melting in a wave that was part hunger, part deep tenderness.

She whispered his name as his lips brushed the aching peaks. His hair was thick and crisp under her hands, and she was barely conscious of inflicting any pain as she knotted her fingers in it, moaning shakily as his tongue firmed her nipples into increasingly unbearable tautness, leaving her soul aching and full, ready for love.

When she thought she could stand it no longer, Cameron drew back, pulling off his shirt so that his magnificent torso was naked in the sunlight. He drew her against the warmth of his skin, cradling her in his arms with possessive strength, his mouth fastening on hers with a force that plunged her into a new abyss of dizziness. Yet his arms were gentle, as though he knew instinctively how boneless and weak she felt. It was intensely sweet to be pressed so close to him, her breasts against his hard chest, her honey against his bronze . . .

'How did we manage to last so long?' he asked huskily, covering her mouth with kisses so that she could not have answered him, even if she'd been able to. Rio was aware of her loins melting hotly, her sexuality becoming ready for him in a way she had never known before.

He cupped her breast in his palm, his thumb caressing the erect nipple again and again, making her arch against him as though some potent drug had been poured into her veins. Her own hands were shameless, hungrily caressing the contours of Cameron's body, tracing the sinews of his throat and shoulders, the hard, flat power of his chest. His nipples were hard and pointed under her palms, his stomach muscled like a Greek god's, the dark hair of his body emphasising his potent maleness.

And beneath the rough denim of his jeans, his manhood was hard and swollen. Her touch there was more accidental than deliberate, but the gasp it drew from deep in his chest thrilled her with knowledge of his arousal.

It was Cameron who drew back at last, his breathing ragged and unsteady. The skin was flushed on his high cheekbones, his eyes a deep stormy blue, more like the sea's depths than the sky's height.

'This isn't the place, Rio.' He brushed the golden hair away from her pink-stained cheeks. 'And it isn't the time. We must stop now.'

'But why?' she moaned, her desire for him aching at its peak.

'Because I'm being a criminal fool.' She arched her neck as he kissed the tender hollow of her throat, turmoil filling her mind.

'Dear heaven,' she whispered, 'it's too late to stop now, my love . . .'

'Almost too late,' he said roughly. 'But not quite.' He drew her close, for comfort this time, not out of passion. Rio clenched her fingers in his thick, dark hair, her body shaking with tortured passion. 'Cameron, don't do this to me!'

'Do you hate me?' he asked, smiling gently at her frantic expression.

'Hate you?' She caressed his face with trembling fingers, and shook her tousled head. 'Never, never, my love——'

'Then let's go now. Before it really *is* too late.'

She hung her head in uncomprehending misery as he fastened her blouse for her. 'I don't understand,' she whispered.

'You will,' he promised, and kissed her hot cheek. 'Besides, it would be sacrilege to make love in a churchyard.'

'We're not in the churchyard,' she said with unhappy practicality, but she could see from his face that it was pointless to argue. With massive strength, Cameron had got his passion under control. It was bitterly unfair, but there was nothing she could do about it.

With despair, Rio realised that she had to be adult now, and match his composure, if she wanted to retain his respect.

Nevertheless, it took a supreme effort to rise on shaky legs, and brush the grass from her rumpled clothes. At least she now knew that his desire matched her own. Whatever reasons he had for stopping now, she'd seen the desire flaming in his eyes, had known his arousal.

And his response had shown her one magical lesson—
that his feelings might not be so very far from her own.
That there was some hope, at least, for her love!

Weak as a kitten, Rio let him help her into the leather
saddle. The ride back was hardly going to help the
dragging pain in her loins, and she would almost rather
have walked, if she'd had the strength. He smiled across at
her as they started the steep ride back to Barramundi,
handsome as the devil. 'I'll never forget this day,' she said
quietly.

'No.' His blue eyes held hers. 'Nor will I.'

But as they rode back through the seas of rippling grass
Rio's new-found sense of self-confidence ebbed steadily
away. It was a classic female mistake to confuse a man's
sexual desire with emotional commitment. That he'd
wanted her body didn't mean he also wanted her love.

And the fact that Cameron had stopped on the brink of
making love to her had only one reasonable interpretation.

That he was trying to spare her. That he knew he could
never love her, and wanted to avoid an entanglement
which he might soon want to sever. For ever.

The wind tugged Rio's hat away from her shoulders, the
ribbon pulling tight across her throat, emphasising the
lump that had formed there. Finish your report, she told
herself bitterly. Get it finished, girl—and then run all the
way back home. From this illusory, golden paradise to the
cold grey reality of your real life.

CHAPTER EIGHT

OBEYING her own dictate, Rio finished her fourth chapter
in an intense burst of activity over the next week. Working
from the precious notebooks she'd salvaged from the

cottage—now sea-stained and creased, but still legible—
she'd been able to rebuild the text she'd lost around the
skeleton of bare figures and measurements.

Soon she was going to get to the stage where she would
need to take account of the damage done by the cyclone;
and that would require a return visit to the cottage.

Still excited by the progress she had made, she brought
the subject up over lunch, which had been served, as usual,
on the ground-floor veranda, overlooking the sea. In
deference to the magnificent lobster dish which the cook
had prepared, Rio had conveniently shelved her principles—as she all too often did these days!

'There won't be anywhere for you to sleep,' Cameron
warned. 'You'll have to take a tent. How long will you
need?'

'Three or four days,' Rio guessed. She finished her last
morsel of diced lobster, reflecting that the period away
from Barramundi might be highly beneficial. It would at
least give her a chance to regain her emotional balance,
away from Cameron's overwhelming presence. 'It'll be odd
being back there,' she mused, chin in hand. 'Sometimes I
feel that I've lived at Barramundi all my life.'

'I'll take that as a compliment,' Cameron smiled. 'When
do you want to go?'

'I thought next Sunday,' she told him.

'I'll ask the kitchen to get some food ready for you to
take,' he nodded, 'and I'll see that the Land Rover's ready
for the drive. You remember the route?'

'I'm not a baby,' she smiled.

'No,' he agreed. 'But I'll miss you for those three or four
days.'

His eyes met hers, and something in them brought a flush
to her cheeks. Since that afternoon up on Grey Mare Hill,
relations between them had been extraordinarily sensitive—a strange mixture of tender warmth and mutual
caution.

She did everything in her power to avoid touching him, for the slightest brush of her skin against his was enough to bring the hot blood rushing to her cheeks. She had also avoided being alone with him as far as she could; and, although they had ridden together each evening, there had been no more walks together, and no more afternoons on the yacht.

'How are your precious sharks?' she asked, breaking the silence shyly.

'Fascinating as ever,' he replied. 'But very problematic.'

'You're not making headway?' she questioned, as servants materialised to clear the table, and bring out a huge bowl of tropical fruit.

'There are several ideas that work very well,' Cameron smiled, 'in a fifty-foot tank. In particular, there are chemicals which will keep sharks at bay, but the problem is that in the sea they'll disperse far too rapidly to do much good. Things which vibrate in the water, or even give them mild electric shocks, just arouse their curiosity, which is literally fatal.' He sliced a papaya in two, scooped out the black seeds, and passed her half. The fruit was delicious with a squeeze of lemon; cool, sweet and exotic.

'What's the answer, then?' Rio asked, her mouth full.

'The research has been valuable,' he shrugged. 'I intend to publish it anyhow, just for its scientific interest. As to the idea of providing defences against shark attacks, I think the simplest solution is going to be to concentrate on lighter and more adaptable cages for divers to work in.'

Rio looked up quickly. 'You sound as though your research is nearly over,' she said in a quiet voice.

'There are still a few last avenues to try,' he told her. 'But you're right. I'm going to start winding it down soon.'

A sick feeling invaded the pit of Rio's stomach. 'And then?' she asked anxiously. 'Will you go back to London?'

Again, his eyes met hers briefly. 'I don't have any immediate plans to go,' he replied, dismissing the idea.

'I see,' she said, but the chill remained. What was there to keep him here, now that his research was coming to an end? It was like hearing the first chimes of doom.

'I take it your work's over for the day?' he asked, throwing down his napkin.

Rio nodded absently. 'I'm not going to do any more.'

'I thought I'd take the yacht up the coast, to the next cove,' he said casually. 'It's quite deserted, and there are some interesting tidal pools along the reef, with some quite rare fauna in them.' He paused with expert timing. 'Care to come?'

It was an invitation that might have been tailor-made to be irresistible to Rio. 'It sounds marvellous,' she smiled.

'A few years back, I made a study there,' he went on. 'It's a unique place, and to my knowledge no one's ever set foot there. I'd like to see how it's all changed.'

'I'll come,' she decided eagerly. 'I'd better go and put my costume on.'

Cameron nodded, and watched her dance out of the room.

Upstairs, she changed into her bikini, pulling on cut-off denims and a T-shirt over it. The prospect of spending an idyllic afternoon among rock-pools with Cameron was warmly exciting. Besides, she told herself, she deserved a break. She'd been working hard this week. Collecting a big fluffy pink towel and goggles, she went back down to meet Cameron.

'Mr Frazer's in the study,' Joseph, the major-domo, told her as she came down. She walked through the hall to the study, following the sound of Cameron's deep voice, talking, she guessed, to one of the servants.

But there was no servant in the room. Instead, he was seated at the wide desk, staring out at the garden, the telephone receiver in his hand.

'Well, put him on,' he was saying impatiently, 'I'll speak to him myself.'

She stood silently in the doorway, listening to the clipped tones of his voice. The conversation was highly technical, evidently about some complex issue of company business. She'd never heard him sound like this before, his voice holding a note of command that was brusque and authoritative. When he rasped, 'Well, for God's sake, can't you take care of it?' Rio felt a pang of pity for whoever it was he was talking to.

Nor did he seem very pleased with what he was hearing; the impatience was creeping audibly into his voice, his long, tanned fingers drumming a devil's tattoo on the leather top.

'Damn it, Rowley,' he snapped at last, 'you're not a child! You don't need me there to hold your hand and tell you what to do!' The other person spoke for a few seconds, and then Cameron sighed in exasperation. 'No, I do *not* have any plans to fly back this month. You and the board will just have to handle it together. It's well within your capabilities. I really don't see what good my presence in London would do.'

He stared unseeingly through the window as he listened for a short while longer, then nodded briefly.

'Good. That's more like it. Call me back when you've got it sorted out. Right? Give my love to Eloise. Take care, Rowley.'

He put the receiver down, and swung on the chair to face her, traces of anger fading from his eyes. 'Why are some men such born panickers?' he demanded.

Rio smiled slightly. The tenor of the call had been only too clear to her. 'You're playing truant,' she told him in a quiet voice. 'It's natural that they're going to panic without you, Cameron.'

He gave her a filthy look, grunted and rose from the chair, tall and straight against the light. 'There's no point in success if it just becomes a ball and chain,' he said shortly. 'Let's get down to the yacht.'

'Why *are* you staying away?' she asked, not moving from her position by the door. 'It's so out of character for you to just abandon your career like this. You've already been here for four months,' she pointed out.

There was a flare of blue anger in his eyes. 'Now, don't you start on me, Rio,' he warned her grimly.

'It must be a pretty good reason,' she pressed, unwilling to let it go.

'It is,' he retorted. 'I like it here.' His brows lowered. 'I notice that *you* don't seem so keen to leave Barramundi either.'

'I'm different,' she said serenely. 'I've got my report to write up before I go home. Anyway, I've nothing to hurry back for, except the prospect of job-hunting and unemployment. You've got a great big company waiting for you, with heaven knows how many commitments——'

'They can cope,' he said shortly.

'I just feel so guilty,' she said, shaking her head.

'Guilty?' he echoed. 'What about?'

'I can't help feeling that I'm one of the reasons that's keeping you away from London,' she sighed. 'Maybe I should pack up and go down to Brisbane, after all——'

He reached out to where a beautifully painted aboriginal boomerang hung on the wall. 'One more word,' he threatened with mock-menace, 'and I'll throw this at you.'

'It'll only fly back into your own face,' Rio said calmly.

He was with her in a stride, arms coming round her to lift her easily off her feet. 'Then I'll throw *you*, instead,' he smiled. His strength took her breath away, thrilling her. 'One more word about going to Brisbane, and you'll be upside down in the flowerbeds.'

'I'll stop,' she promised in a quavering voice. 'Just put me down!'

'Good.' He kissed her mouth hard before he released her. 'Are we going for this sail, then, or not?'

* * *

They moored the yacht a safe distance off the beach, and Cameron rowed the dinghy into the shallows. It was one of the most beautiful places Rio had ever seen: a curving rind of pure white sand, stretching into a shallow intertidal zone of reefs, shoals, and pools. It was sheltered by high sandbanks on the landward side, and by the Great Barrier Reef on the seaward side.

The sky was cloudless overhead, and the sun was bakingly hot. She could hardly wait to strip down to her bikini and wade through the warm shallows with Cameron, peering into the tidal pools and marvelling at the vast variety of marine life thriving in the warm, clear water.

'During the spring tides, these pools are cut off from the sea for very long periods,' he told her, as he helped her over a slippery reef. 'The temperature of the water soars, and so does the salinity—while the oxygen level drops to practically nil. It's a miracle that these creatures survive at all. I wrote a paper about it once, pointing out that the coral fauna don't seem to mind extremes of temperatures which are supposed to kill them.'

'You probably know more about corals than I do,' Rio said wryly. She sent him a quick glance from under her fringe of golden hair. 'Remember when I asked you whether you'd noticed the Great Barrier Reef?'

He grinned at the memory, and led her down to a blood-warm turquoise pool that was bright with striped fish and the weaving, multi-coloured arms of sea anemones. He was naked but for the narrow black strip of his costume, its sheer nylon barely containing his manhood. It was difficult to keep her eyes off his body; he was so magnificently male, his long black hair tumbling almost to his shoulders, the perfectly formed muscles moving in waves beneath his bronzed skin.

Was she a hopeless wanton, to worship his body like this? She'd always been taught it was unfeminine to notice a man's physical attributes. Then a soft smile curved her

mouth as she recalled that line from the wedding service
'With my body, I thee worship . . .'

They squatted at the edge of the pool, soaking up the sun
while Rio vainly tried to manoeuvre her little net round
one of the striped fish, which were of a species she didn't
recognise. She was hopelessly slow, so he took it from her,
and in a short while had netted two of the little creatures.

'Clownfish,' he said, holding them up for her to look at.
'They hide among the sea anemones—apparently, the
poison doesn't affect them.' Rio studied the fish for a while,
then released them, and watched them flick towards the
nearest clump of sea anemones and burrow into the waving
tentacles, bearing out Cameron's identification of them.

Further out, where the pools grew much bigger, they
were able to dive. Rio had always much preferred
snorkelling to the fuss and bother of scuba-diving, enjoying
the freedom of not having weights and heavy air-bottles to
contend with. To her, it was utter bliss to simply float on the
surface, breathing easily through the plastic tube, and
watching the teeming undersea life below her.

Cameron had lent her his waterproof Nikon—her own
underwater camera had been lost at the cottage—and she
used it to record anything that was new to her, or especially
lovely.

Occasionally, they would kick down to the bottom, to
look at something particularly interesting from close by;
and Rio's net-bag was soon bulging with the beautiful shells
she'd been collecting. The absence of pounding waves
among these miniature lagoons ensured that even the most
delicate shells remained unbroken.

She showed Cameron a particularly lovely cone-shell, so
delicate that its curved sides were translucent.

'Beautiful,' he nodded, his dark hair slicked back by the
water.

'The surf was so heavy at the cottage that these were
always pounded to fragments,' she marvelled. 'Only the

heaviest and hardest shells used to survive.'

He smiled at her enthusiasm. 'There's a big colony of corals over there,' he invited. She followed him to the seaward end of the pool, towing her bag of shells behind her. As he'd promised, it was a spectacular outcrop, on a sloping bank a few feet down, mostly consisting of dark brown brain-corals.

'*Platygyra*.' She identified the strange and beautiful creatures unhesitatingly. 'That really is a wonderful sight.'

'I thought you'd like it.'

They dived down to the colony, and Rio noted the crystal-clear, warm water that would have favoured this particularly good formation. She photographed it from several angles with the Nikon—then, for good measure, took a couple of shots of Cameron, sitting on a reef and grinning down at her.

The afternoon drifted by in golden peace. By early evening the sun was low, and the fierce heat of the day had started to subside. Salty and tired, Rio climbed into the dinghy, and Cameron rowed them out to the yacht.

It's teak decks were blood-warm underfoot, and though Rio hardly ever drank alcohol, there was somthing very tempting about his offer of a sundowner on the foredeck.

'This is *definitely* the life,' she sighed contentedly, subsiding into a deckchair, and leaning back to watch the glorious sunset over the bay.

'You should have been born a hundred years ago,' Cameron smiled, passing her a cool gin and orange, and relaxing in the chair beside her. 'Gin slings at sunset—quite *de rigueur*, my love.'

He stretched out his long, muscular legs, the black strip of his costume pulling tight in a way that made her avert her gaze with a hot prickle of self-consciousness.

'Except that I would never have been able to lie around in a bikini,' she pointed out. She fished the slice of orange out of her drink, and sucked it thoughtfully. 'I feel so sorry for those Victorian women, cocooned in so many clothes, and in this climate, too. It must have been torture to go down to the beach, all swaddled in crinolines and a bonnet, and half a dozen petticoats, not to mention button boots— and wish you were paddling naked in the surf . . .'

'No,' he said thoughtfully, studying her brown figure beside him, 'I don't think your bikini would have met with great-grandmother's approval at all.'

'Is it unsuitable?' she asked anxiously, looking down at herself.

'It's ravishing,' he assured her. 'I just find it rather a strain having to watch you in it. Or out of it, as the case may be.'

The colour touched her cheeks at the expression in his eyes, which was unmistakably warm and appreciative. 'I wish I hadn't lost my one-piece at the cottage,' she said regretfully, wriggling in her chair.

'I don't,' he assured her. 'That would have spoiled my fun.'

'I didn't know you'd noticed,' she replied, trying to match the calmness of the sunset sky.

'I notice everything you wear,' he said gently. 'Or do. Or say.' His eyes drifted over the pink triangle of nylon between her slim thighs. 'And it suits you very well— Royale,'

'Thank you,' she said, definitely flustered now. 'But whoever owned this was a different shape from me.'

'I think you're right,' he said with the ghost of a smile.

She sent him an assessing glance from under her long lashes. 'Whose *was* it, anyway?' she asked lightly.

He shrugged broad shoulders. 'It belonged to some female visitor at Barramundi.'

'Some female visitor with excellent taste.' She peeled the bottom down an inch to show him the Christian Dior label. 'She didn't leave any other clothes behind, by any chance?'

His eyes studied her smooth, exposed skin for a moment.

'As it happens, I really don't remember too much about her,' he said, retreating behind what she always thought of as his Cheshire-cat smile.

'Were there so many, then?' she asked innocently. 'Or was this one particularly undistinguished?'

'Put your claws back in, pussycat.'

'You're remarkably discreet about your conquests,' Rio smiled, though she was only half teasing. 'You must have had women falling around you ever since you were sixteen.'

'Fourteen,' he corrected her gravely.

'Fourteen! Is that when you——' She choked on the question, cursing herself for swallowing the bait. 'And in the back of a car, too,' she finished, her voice holding just the right note of shocked disapproval.

His laugh was soft and rich. 'If you really want to know about my sex-life, I've had my share—but I've never been promiscuous. And the previous owner of that bikini was *not* one of my conquests.'

'Good,' Rio said unhesitatingly. 'Though she must have been undistinguished indeed—considering that you like it so much on me.'

He glanced at her again. 'She didn't fill it out in quite the way you do,' he volunteered.

'I do seem to have put on so much weight,' she mourned, looking down at herself. 'I've never been as fat as this. It must be all that lobster. I knew I should have stuck to my vegetarian diet.'

'Eating some proper food, instead of that soya-bean rubbish, has done you the world of good,' he replied. 'You've blossomed at Barramundi.'

'Blossomed into a cactus flower,' she retorted. 'Fat and fleshy.'

'You're not fat in the slightest,' he said softly. 'If you're fishing for compliments, Rio, you happen to be the most completely desirable woman I've ever set eyes on.'

His words, and the velvety tone they were delivered in,

brought the blood rushing to Rio's cheeks. Hotly embarrassed, yet also utterly delighted by the compliment, she drained her glass, hoping that the cool drink would bring down her inner temperature.

'It's been a lovely, unforgettable afternoon,' she sighed at last, smiling across at him. 'Thank you for giving it to me.'

'Thank you for being here. I wanted to share this place with you. I knew you would appreciate it.'

They watched the huge disc of the sun as it sank lower, staining the sky with crimson. It was a spectacle of great and serene beauty, and Rio couldn't help thinking of another sunset they'd watched together, such a long, long time ago now. As if he'd picked up her thoughts exactly, Cameron smiled gently.

'I don't think I've ever been so glad to see the sun as on that day. There was a time when I thought we might not live to see it again.'

'Were you really afraid during the cyclone?' she asked, grey eyes widening in surprise.

'"Pessimistic" would be a better word,' he said drily. 'It wasn't exactly a reassuring situation.'

'But you had such an aura of calm strength,' Rio marvelled. 'I was absolutely sure you'd get us through it!'

'I'm very good at calm strength,' Cameron smiled mischievously.

'If I'd known you didn't rate our chances, I'd have collapsed on the spot!'

'Which is why I didn't let you know,' he pointed out.

Rio shook her head with a smile. 'The longer I know you, the more devious I realise you are, Cameron.'

'When you've realised that I'm totally devious,' he glinted, 'then you'll *really* understand me.' He drained his glass, then smiled at her with warm eyes. 'We've got to know each other rather well, haven't we?'

'I think you know me well,' she replied. 'As to whether I really know you . . .' Rio's voice tailed off for a moment as she looked into the ruby orb of the dying sun. 'Sometimes I think I hardly know you at all.'

'You know me all too well,' Cameron contradicted her. 'Want another drink?'

'That one's gone to my head already,' she declined. 'Can I have a shower before we leave for Barramundi? I'm all salt and sand.'

'So am I. Go on ahead,' he invited. 'I'll take one when you're finished. In the meantime, I'll tidy the deck up.'

In the downstairs cabin, Rio stripped off the contentious bikini, and dropped it in the hand-basin to soak. The sight of that Dior label brought a quick smile to her soft lips, then she stepped into the shower cubicle, and reached for the tap.

The balmy evening air was warm enough to make the pure water deliciously refreshing on her naked skin. She luxuriated under the steady stream, letting the salt drain away from her hair, leaving her skin clean and sweet.

It had been a day of marvellous closeness with Cameron, filled with beauty and joy.

A sharp pang went through her to think that there was any life beyond this. This was like being in the garden before the fall, a garden full of wonders and delights, and with such an Adam as even her sweetest dreams could not have supplied . . .

She reached for the soap with a slow sigh, and began lathering her thighs and hips, her mind filled with bright images of him, and the day's events.

'I've just remembered something important.'

The deep voice made her turn quickly, eyes widening in surprise as she clutched the soap to her breasts. Cameron was sliding into the cubicle with her, deep blue eyes glittering with wicked amusement.

'Wha—what——'

'I forgot to fill the tanks this morning,' he said, pulling the curtain shut behind him. His lithe nakedness brushed hers as he claimed a place in the spray. 'There's only enough fresh water for one shower.' He eased the slippery cake of soap out of her clutching fingers. 'So we'll have to share,' he informed her.

She couldn't help the giggle that rose in her throat. 'Ah, well,' she gurgled, 'we've seen each other naked before, I suppose.'

'Quite,' he said calmly. and started soaping her smooth shoulders with expert fingers.

'What are you doing?' she said breathlessly.

'Washing you, of course,' he said, quirking an eyebrow at the obvious question. His closeness was sending her blood pressure soaring way up into the danger-zone, but she was too taken aback to speak, let alone protest at the dangerous game Cameron was playing. When he leaned forward to kiss her wet mouth, she felt the powerful length of his hard, naked body against her own.

Rio closed her eyes helplessly as he soaped her with erotic thoroughness. There was an almost shockingly intense sensual pleasure in feeling his hands on her skin, spreading the creamy lather across her shoulders, down her arms, then up the smooth ridges of her ribcage, to the swell of her breasts.

She couldn't bite back her gasp as he cupped her breasts, soaping them with possessive gentleness, massaging their full curves, his thumbs circling her soft nipples with slow strokes, until she felt them tighten and stand out, intensifying in pleasure until she melted against him, whispering his name in a plea for mercy.

If it had started as a game, it was suddenly a game no longer. She clung to him, her lips blindly seeking his. His tongue invaded her mouth hotly, and then their bodies were pressed together, stomach to stomach, thigh to thigh. Her blood pounded wildly through her veins as she responded to his kiss, her hands caressing his wet body with shameless hunger. He was all hard muscle, from broad shoulders to the taut, sinewy thighs that strained against her; all hers, completely and without reservations.

This time, she prayed silently, let there be no stopping half-way. She had never been so ready for love, had never needed fulfilment so urgently or fiercely.

Oblivious to the streaming water, they kissed with the insatiable hunger of lovers, Rio's emotion surging wildly as she felt Cameron's arousal against her loins, hard and searing.

She barely noticed as the shower's stream slowed to a trickle, then stopped altogether, but Cameron drew back, and looked down at her with dark eyes. 'I told you there wasn't much water left,' he said, his voice thick with passion. 'I'm afraid I didn't get all of you washed . . .'

'I don't think I could have stood it anyway,' she whispered, nestling in his arms.

He pushed the shower-curtain aside, and led her to the bunk, seating her. Feeling that she was melting with desire for him, Rio sat on the edge of the bed and watched him as he picked up the soft, fluffy towel, then came to kneel on the floor in front of her.

'I'd better dry you before you catch cold,' he said huskily. He looped the oversized towel round her shoulders, and began patting her golden skin dry. While he was doing it, she leaned forward to find his mouth again, her hands cupping his face, feeling the bristle of his beard under her fingers.

Now their kisses were more languorous, their caresses more deliberate. She had looked into the potent depths of those blue eyes, and had seen that this time there would be no holding back.

That knowledge had both thrilled and calmed her. There was no longer any hurry between them, only the desire to give without reservation, to fulfil their physical passion, and consummate the love that had been growing so strongly between them for so long.

They explored one another's mouths with slow sensuality, losing themselves in the depth of the kiss, until Cameron's hands forgot to dry her skin any longer, but encircled her with growing tightness.

'Rio,' he whispered, kissing her slender throat, his hands cupping the curve of her hips, 'I've wanted you so much today. I've hardly been able to take my eyes off you, my love. You're so lovely that it makes my heart ache to watch you . . .'

She was too full of emotion to speak, but the expression on her face told him everything. He laughed quietly, not needing any words, and dried the last of the water from her body.

In a kind of trance, Rio watched the muscles of his shoulders swell and relax as he moved. The man kneeling before her was quite simply the most beautiful human being she had ever seen, a combination of strength, grace and power that took her breath away. The miracle was that she seemed to overwhelm him with the same emotions, because she could see the same adoration in his face as he caressed her woman's body in the fluffy folds of the pink towel.

He merely had to lean forward to cover the erect peaks of her breasts with his mouth, drawing a whimper from her as she felt his tongue answer her yearning, his teeth nipping the rosy flesh with sensuous cruelty.

'You're so beautiful, Cameron,' she whispered, 'and I need you so!'

Her spine arched under his hands as his mouth trailed down her belly, his tongue probing the neat cleft of her navel, tracing the silky pathways of pleasure across her body.

Under her caressing hands, Cameron's hair was thick and wet, the black curls knotting round her fingers as though it were a living part of him, deliberately drawing her to the erotic brink of their passion.

With my body, I thee worship . . .

The words drifted through her mind like a poem as she felt his warm kisses on the sensitive flesh of her thighs, his mouth making its way to the melting centre of her need with unashamed hunger.

Rio was too shy at first to admit him; and then there was no longer a choice.

The caress of his tongue lifted her to a new plateau of passion. She was conscious, as she moaned aloud, of an almost physical sensation of soaring flight—and yet there could be nothing more physical, more earthy than the way he was kissing her now; and the flickering, teasing pleasure she'd felt up till now burst into a bonfire that consumed any last vestiges of the inhibition that might have lingered between them.

She sank back, the bones seeming to melt within her limbs. At the point where it became too much to bear, he rose from between her thighs, and came to her side on the bed.

Her throat was dry and speechless as she looked up at Cameron, the grey of her eyes turned to silver by his love.

'My dear, dear one,' he whispered, leaning over her, 'you know there's been no woman in my life like you, don't you?'

'Oh, Cameron . . .'

'I've wanted you for so long,' he went on, brushing the wet strands of hair away from the heart-shaped oval of her face. 'It's been a torment to be so close to you, day after day, and to restrain myself from touching you as I wanted to. From the first moment I saw you, I knew I'd make love to you some day.' He smiled gently. 'But I'd always imagined it would be on silken sheets, with roses and champagne. I should have known better.'

He kissed her face, his mouth moving from her lips to her eyelids, across the peach-blossom skin, across the wet curls of her hair, in the shell-like curl of her ear.

The deep crimson glow of the sunset flooded the little cabin, bathing them both in its dying light, but neither noticed. She no longer needed light to see him by—she was in a world where touch and taste and smell reigned supreme.

She could only whisper his name, as he continued his worship of her. But not like any man had ever done before. There was no hurry in Cameron's desire, none of the rush and guilt she'd felt in her previous lovers. Nor, despite the potency of his need for her, did she sense that selfish concentration on his own pleasure which had alientated her so much from the men she'd known at Oxford.

Instead, he was focused on her, as though, to Cameron, sex meant *her* delight, rather than his. The dizzying expertise of his mouth and hands told her he'd made love to many, many women before her, and yet she didn't consider that now. She'd believed him utterly when he'd told her she was special to him, and that precious knowledge burned in her heart now, turning the simple act of love into a consummation that was almost spiritual.

Nothing mattered but his touch, as gentle at first as the warm sun itself. He kissed her mouth as though it were a flower, his hands exploring the curves and hollows of her body, arousing desires that had lain hidden all her life, seeming to know Rio's body better than she knew it herself.

Her thighs parted to admit his caress, and she moaned as he cupped the mound of her womanhood, the intimacy of his touch bringing a new dimension to her pleasure, an intensity that almost disorientated her senses, as though her body were melting hotly, changing elements into something fluid and weightless.

He was a sophisticated, aware lover, his gentleness and skill lifting their union way, way above the purely animal coupling she'd known before him. With a profound inner delight, Rio realised that this was what sex ought to be. For the first time in her life, she was achieving the heights to which lovemaking could rise between a senstive woman and a potent, intelligent man.

Cameron had been almost relaxed, almost poised until now; but as she arched in his arms, whimpering at the long, slow caress across the aching peak of her desire, she sensed his arousal flare into a white heat.

Her own hand had trailed across the inside of his thigh, her fingers curling to trap his manhood and feel the potent strength with which it rose from his loins and thrust to her. Now she answered his caress, feeling his desire grow and charge itself for her. She could not bear it for much longer; she needed Cameron, needed all of him, now.

'Please,' she begged him, 'please, my love . . .'

'I've been waiting my whole life for this,' he whispered. 'Tonight you are mine, all of you . . .'

He slid on to her, his hips parting her thighs, and found the entrance to her body with slow, loving gentleness, without greed or roughness. At the moment he entered her, Rio felt a sense of possession, of completion, that flooded her soul.

The liquid smoothness of her own body admitted his potency to the final limit, until there was no space between them, no inch of their skins that seemed not to be touching.

He made no movement for a long while, just held her tight in his arms. Rio clung to him, her face buried against his throat, as she'd clung to him during a different kind of storm. When he drew back quietly to look into her eyes, she thought with distant wonder that this man had been a stranger to her a few bare weeks ago. Now he was making love to her with a mature, generous skill that was beyond anything she'd ever known.

She looked up at him with misty grey eyes, her face dewy and soft.

'Am I hurting you?' he asked softly, kissing her moist lips.

'No,' she whispered. His mouth claimed hers again as he

began to move, deep inside her, at first with such gentleness
that she arched in frustration, then with increasing power,
forcing her to respond with her own hips, to exchange the
deep pleasure of their lovemaking. She was drowning in a
sea of sweet pleasure, her desire no longer localised, but
flooding her whole body with warmth.

It was too intense to last long. The waves grew stronger
and more potent, rocking her senses, until the end came.
With a sense of utter union with him, she arched upwards,
and together they cried out in an eruption of release that
was close to pain, and yet so beautiful that Rio's eyes were
filled with tears as she clung to him, and sobs choked her
throat.

In the exquisite aftermath of their lovemaking, Cameron
lay at her side, kissing her face and body with unceasing
tenderness, as though no single act of love could slake the
need he felt for her. She lay in his arms, stroking his velvety
skin, just soaking her spirit in this surfeit of love.

'Did you mean it?' she whispered drowsily, looking up at
him with drugged eyes.

'Mean what?' Cameron smiled down at her.

'That there's never been a woman in your life like me...'

'Every word,' he promised, sealing her lips with his own.
In the wake of passion, his face was tender, the smile that
curved his magnificent mouth, gentle. 'Is that the way you
feel about me?' he murmured.

She shook her head in amused disapproval. 'You don't
have to ask that, Cameron. There have been other men, yes.
But nothing remotely, faintly, glimmeringly, like you.' She
captured the hand that was caressing the swell of her
breasts, and kissed the tanned knuckles. 'I've never been
much good ... in bed.'

'Not until now,' he corrected her in amusement.

'I didn't know what making love meant until now,' she
told him seriously. 'I used to think it was all ... overrated.'

He tilted one black eyebrow. 'And now?' he enquired.

She just smiled up at him, so lovely that he caught his breath, and bent to kiss her again. She slid an arm round his neck, her mouth close to his ear. 'Did you expect more from me?' she asked softly. 'I know so little . . .'

'Idiot,' he growled, sharp teeth punishing her insecurity, making her yelp. He drew back. 'Your beauty always stunned me, Rio. Now I know that you're beautiful——' His hand moved in a caress so intimate that she moaned aloud. '—everywhere,' he finished with a wicked grin. 'I'm going to hoist the sails, little one. If we don't get back soon, Joseph will be sending up distress flares.'

He drew the sheet over her, kissed her once more, then rolled her on to her side. She wanted to protest, but the languorous relaxtion in her limbs was too delicious to resist.

'I'll see you later,' he whispered in her ear, '. . . darling.'

Rio smiled as she curled up, hugging the pillow, her heavy eyelids closing over her eyes. A little while later, she heard the distant whirr of the winches, and then the gentle movement of the yacht turning to sail down the coast, home to Barramundi. Her whole being was concentrated on her love for Cameron, on the place in her heart that he had filled for ever, on the sweet ache inside her body where he had been.

Yes, she loved him. Loved him with a totality that caught up her whole being. There had been no one like him before, and there would never be anyone like him again. She knew that with complete certainty, a certainty which took away all worry, all doubt from her mind. After all, nothing else really mattered.

She slept.

Cameron's gentle kiss lifted her from the deep, deep ocean of her sleep, much later in the evening.

'We're home,' he murmured, sitting beside her. She rolled over into his arms. Her naked breasts brushed against cloth; he was wearing a polo-necked shirt and jeans.

Her lips parted under his kiss, deep and loving, until the first flicker of new desire ignited in her.

'You'd better get dressed, Royale,' he smiled. 'Unless you want to walk into the house as naked as the day you were born.' He switched on the bedside lamp, filling the cabin with soft yellow light.

'I was dreaming of you,' she sighed as she clambered out of the bunk, her body feeling marvellously light and free.

'I've been dreaming of you all the way back,' he told her. He held out the lacy scrap of her panties, and sat on the bunk she'd just vacated, to watch her dress, with dark, desirious eyes.

'Why are you looking at me like that?' she asked, shaking the golden hair out of her eyes.

'You know why,' he said gently.

She threw him a soft smile. 'Yes. I suppose I do.' For the first time, Rio was taking a deep pleasure in having a man watch her body, in knowing that the sight of her was arousing him. She moved with innate grace, and as she arched her back to pull on her shirt, she was rewarded by hearing him whisper her name, and seeing him move to her like a panther, taking her in his arms, and kissing the dark nipples that had been flaunted so provocatively at him.

'Cameron,' she cried huskily, 'I don't want this to end. Not ever.'

'Come on,' he growled fiercely at last, 'we'll continue this in the house.'

The night was warm and moonless, and the air was sweet with the fragrance of the flowers in the garden. The darkness only emphasised the lights of Barramundi up above the jetty. The windows blazed like jewels in the night, calling a welcome to them.

Clinging together, they walked across the gangplank, and through the scented garden, towards the great house.

CHAPTER NINE

'Do you really have to go?' growled Cameron, his mouth close against her ear.

'If I don't go back to the cottage tomorrow, I'll never go,' Rio said, and knew it was the truth. 'Besides, it's all been settled, my love, ages ago.'

Cameron grunted in dissatisfaction, his arms still tight round her. She laid her golden head against his shoulder, praying that he'd never want to let her go. Her need for him had become all-consuming in this past week, a hunger that was as vital to her as breathing. If he ever left her, she'd be torn apart, bereaved . . .

'I wish I was coming with you,' he grumbled, and kissed her temple tenderly. 'I hate the thought of you spending four days all alone there, in a tent.'

'I spent six weeks there,' she remined him mischievously, 'and you never even summoned up the interest to come and see me once.'

'You weren't exactly welcoming when I *did* arrive,' Cameron pointed out drily. 'I'll never forget the frosty look in those beautiful grey eyes, when you saw me standing on your beach.'

'I was a different person, then,' she said simply. 'I'm not the same Royale Faber any more, Cameron. I'm yours, now.'

'Then I command you not to go to the cottage,' he smiled.

'You know you'll release me from that command.' They'd been embracing in the shade of the Pride of India tree at the bottom of the garden, and now they kissed once more, and walked back towards the house together. The late afternoon sun cast long shadows across the immaculately manicured lawn. 'I *must* get that new evidence to finish my report,' she went on, lacing her fingers through his. 'And even if you could come with me, I wouldn't get a thing done. We'd just lie on the beach and make love all day.'

'What's wrong with that?' he smiled.

'Oh, love, don't make it any harder for me,' Rio sighed. 'It's going to tear a hole in my heart to leave you anyway. I'll spend every moment thinking of you. But I've got to get it done. I'm on a Cotton Foundation grant, remember? I can't let them down, not when so many people had to compete for that money.'

'Hmmm,' he rumbled, not sounding very convinced. She just smiled to herself. He couldn't possibly know how sweet it was to hear his protests at her leaving Barramundi for four days. To be wanted by him was something more precious than pearls or rubies. She would study the rest of her life to learn how to keep being wanted by Cameron, with that same fiercely possessive need she could see in him now.

The servants they met in the hall beamed at them. There was no question that they were all utterly delighted by what had happened between Rio and their master. If they'd been attentive before she and Cameron had taken that trip up the coast, they were now adoring. Unbidden, there had been masses of flowers on the table at all their meals; and after she'd spent the first two nights with Cameron, all her possessions had been discreetly moved into Cameron's bedroom, as if to emphasise their wish that the change must be permanent.

She'd blushed furiously when she'd realised the implications of what they'd done, but Cameron had been helpless with laughter. 'You don't seem to have much choice but to stay with me,' he'd pointed out. 'Not unless you want to do without your clothes.

And so, after those long, golden weeks of self-control, they'd become lovers, in the true sense of the word.

She had never known a man as loving as Cameron. He

was tender, adoring, a joyous and powerful lover who raised her to the utmost heights of physical passion. But there was so much more to him. He was the first man, Rio was just beginning to recognise, beside whom she had not felt an intellectual superior. His intelligence was towering; and yet it was tempered with a compassion for all living things, a sense of humility, even, which sometimes made her ashamed of her own arrogance.

Every day, she was learning more and more from him. He was leading her now, helping her to fulfil all the promise that had until now been only half realised in her.

It was as though every dislocated piece in Rio's life had imperceptibly clicked together, making her a whole person. Cameron had shown her, for the first time, what happiness really was. Not a passing emotion, not a contentment that faded. It was a state of being, a joy that pervaded every fibre of her life, changing everything.

The world appeared to her in new colours now. When she awoke each morning in Cameron's strong arms, after nights of abandoned and marvellous lovemaking, Rio had a sense of unity with the world that—had another woman described it to her—she would have found very hard to believe a few months ago.

Her life at the cottage had been closed, rather than perfect; she had survived, rather than lived. She could never have understood the meaning of love until now, not by any stretch of her imagination. It was simply too far beyond her experience.

And now it went so deep into her that sometimes it frightened her; and only her total trust in Cameron stopped her from feeling moments of complete helplessness.

They had their evening meal on the veranda, talking in soft tones, holding hands across the table. To Rio, her imminent departure had its bittersweet pleasure—almost excitement, even. He had shown her, at least, how much he wanted her at his side. And, though it would be a supreme test of her will-power to leave him, the thought of his welcoming passion, when she returned after those nights spent apart, made her melt inside.

It was all ready; the Land Rover had been packed for her with a tent, blankets, and enough food to last her a week, at least. She was going to be setting off early in the morning, and would try and get back by Wednesday night.

'I'll be fine,' she promised him over the fruit that ended their meal. 'I really will. I'm not nearly as delicate as I look.'

'I've learned that by now,' he nodded wryly. 'Still, I would really have preferred to come with you.'

'Who are these people you're waiting for?' Rio asked.

'Gerald Ross, from the National Aquarium, and his team. They're going to try and transfer the sharks overland to Darwin.'

'The sharks are going into the Aquarium?'

'At first,' he nodded. 'Later, they'll go back to the sea, where they belong.'

She nodded, reflecting that he really was winding his research down now. That meant that by the time her report was finished, in a week or two from now, they would both be ready to return to England. 'Well, don't let them out while I'm down at the cottage,' she smiled, thinking of those sleek, sinister shapes in the pools.

'That's another thing,' he said, blue eyes imperious. 'Don't you ever forget those vital rules. Don't swim if you're bleeding, even from a scratch——'

'Don't thrash around in the water,' she finished for him, 'don't swim if the water's murky, and keep my eyes peeled at all times. I won't forget, I promise!'

'I still think Joseph ought to come with you,' he said broodingly.

'Joseph's got better things to do with his time than sit on the sand and cook oysters over a campfire for me,' she smiled.

'Obstinate woman,' he sighed. But the look he gave her

expressed anything but anger. They rose from the table together.

Cameron put a record on the turntable in the *salon*, a sweet selection of Chopin, and they walked along the veranda, listening to the rhapsodic music, and talking the hours away.

'I never thought four days could seem such a long time,' she mused, when a lull in their conversation brought her thoughts back to the morrow. 'It yawns ahead of me, like a huge chasm.'

'I know what you mean.' He quirked a dark eyebrow at her. 'Which reminds me—ought we really to be wasting time at this point?'

'Why, whatever can you mean, *monsieur*?' she laughed breathlessly.

'Come up to my *boudoir* and I'll show you, *mam'selle*,' he grinned.

In the cool white bedroom, he lit a candle by the side of the bed, and in its flickering, soft light, began to undress her. She felt her blood pounding in her veins as he slowly unfastened the buttons of her dress, his kisses covering her face and throat, and wondered whether he would ever tire of her. But his reaction, as he exposed the perfect curves of her breasts in the candle-light, was thrilling reassuringly— a groan of desire that went to her heart.

He pressed his face against her breasts, holding her tight, and murmuring her name softly. When they kissed, it was with a tenderness that made the blood pound through Rio's veins.

'Make love to me again,' she whispered huskily.

'Yes.' He smiled into her eyes, magnificent and utterly male. 'But not like a stranded starfish, Rio.' He swung to sit cross-legged, and drew her to him, still smiling. 'Like this. I want to look into your eyes,' he said softly, pulling her close, lifting her hips so that she was sitting on his thighs, her knees around his lean waist, her hands clasped round his neck. 'Are you shy?' he murmured gently.

'No,' she whispered shakily. Her need for him was a fierce ache, intensified by the erotic position they were in. With sure hands, he guided her hips forward, sliding her down his thighs until she gasped at the touch of his desire against her, the imminent entry of his body into hers.

'Kiss me,' he commanded roughly.

Her eyes had fluttered shut, and she gave him her mouth, parting her lips for his kiss. And their naked bodies locked together in an embrace without seams.

It was ironic, Rio thought, kicking back up to the surface in a column of bubbles, that after all her detailed observations the most severe damage to the coral bed should have been caused by nature, and not by man.

She floated in the swell of the waves, getting her breath back after the long dive. The damage down there was even more extensive than she'd realised yesterday. At the depth most of the corals grew, the action of waves was usually more or less irrelevant. But the very heavy surf caused by Cyclone Trixie had torn many of the more delicate formations loose, snapping the fragile spires which it had taken years of patient labour to erect.

The surging currents had also rolled massive pieces of rock around, crushing some areas, and had silted other areas beneath deep layers of sand.

It was a woeful sight. Yet, as she dived again now, photographing the damage with Cameron's underwater Nikon, Rio could see that re-growth had already started. New buds were already in the process of forming among the surviving polyps, and new colour was gradually creeping across the bare patches.

Moreover, and most importantly of all, the cylone appeared to have had a dramatic effect on the crown-of-thorns starfish population. Of the grotesque, poisonous creatures, which had been so abundant along this reef, feeding on the coral in their characteristically destructive fashion, hardly a single specimen now remained.

Maybe they had been dragged further out to sea, or perhaps killed by the surge action of the waves. Either way, their numbers had been drastically reduced.

With growing excitement, Rio had realised that in this section of the Barrier Reef, at least, Trixie had swept away one of the major predators on the coral population.

She must tell Cameron of this apparent blessing in disguise, and get his opinion. Swimming back to shore, she reflected that the larvae of the crown-of-thorns starfish were part of the corals' normal diet. It was possible, therefore, that the corals themselves might from now on be able to keep down that gruesome population explosion among the starfish which had made some scientists fear that the days of the reef might be numbered.

Her report was going to have a number of very interesting features!

It might even turn out to be an exceptional piece of work. With luck, at any rate, it would excite sufficient interest to genuinely enhance her chances of getting a job.

And getting a job was still important to her. In a sense, it was extremely unfortunate that Cameron happened to be the head of BTS—because she knew in her heart that if Cameron were to offer her a job with the company, she would be very torn. In the end, she would probably have to refuse. For the sake of her self-respect, she couldn't risk any doubts that she might have been given a job because of her connection with Cameron Frazer. The implication was too ugly.

No, she had to pursue a job legitimately, and with some other company. Because, whichever way things turned out between her and the man she loved, she wanted that crown, delusory though it might be. If he were to ask her to leave work at some future date, perhaps even to marry him, and have his children, that would be different. But she had to forbid herself to think of that. It was a vision too intoxicating, too sweet, to be treated as a mere fantasy.

In the meantime, she had to make up her mind to make no demands on Cameron, to expect nothing beyond the love he gave so freely, and to face the dark possibility that the relationship might not be permanent.

For it *was* a possibility, terrifying and numbing though it seemed. Her fear of that possibility was still latent. If she let it grow, it would become a corroding insecurity that would poison whatever time she and Cameron had left together. But her consciousness of the possibility made her more determined than ever to make a personal success out of her career. Maybe if she did so, when the crash came, she would be better able to face it. Getting a job, in fact, would probably be the most important single bulwark against that day . . .

And finally, it came back to the question of self-respect. Rio had been highly trained, and was highly motivated, and she needed to be able to put that training and motivation to work. Biology, especially marine biology, was a fairly narrow field. It wasn't going to be easy to find a job, but she had to know she was able to do so.

She completed her notes on the beach, thinking how often she had gone through these actions here in the past, and then walked up to her tent, her mind filled with thoughts of Cameron, and their future.

She had pitched the tent a short distance from the cottage. The Foundation had sent someone here while she'd been away, for the site had been cleared of debris, and the heaps of bricks, sand, and cement bags indicated that reconstruction was imminent.

'Make it a bit stronger this time,' she advised the absent builder wryly.

Coming back to this site she was so fond of had made her conscious of just how much she'd changed since the day she'd left it behind her. The Rio Faber who now lit her evening fire, and watched the sun go down beyond the blue hills, was no longer a girl. She was a mature woman in love, a woman infinitely richer in spirit and experience. A stronger woman, far better able to face life than she had been before.

It was pleasantly nostalgic to stare at the familiar scene, and reflect on all the changes that had taken place in her universe recently. Being alone here had brought one thing home to her—that she would never regret what had happened. No matter how much he might hurt her in the future, she would always know that it would never be deliberately. And he had enriched her life immeasurably.

She just prayed that the realisation was not a premonition of any kind.

Thinking about him reminded her that she'd already spent two nights away from Cameron, and she was missing him horribly, and starting to ache for his touch. It was with a sense of real joy that she contemplated her return to Barramundi tomorrow night ...

Just thinking of Cameron had set the hairs on her nape prickling, the fine down on her arms erecting in goose-flesh.

She watched the sun go down, and then the moon rise. She watched the stars appear, one by one at first, like diamonds being set against black velvet, then, as darkness fell, trooping out in glittering hosts. One more night like this, one more night alone, and she would be back with him.

She was dusty and weary by the time she reached Barramundi on Thursday night. The distance was short, even by English terms, but the appalling roads made it seem three times as long, and it had been horribly frustrating to watch the miles creep so reluctantly by.

She'd been tempted to stop at Skewes Bank, a sentimental visit; but her urgent need to get back to Cameron had kept her foot on the accelerator.

As she steered the Land Rover up the long drive, she thought with sybaritic anticipation of the bliss of lying naked on the bed, Cameron's strong hands massaging the ache out of her back.

He was going to be as excited as she was about the crown-of-thorns starfish, she felt sure. And when she'd told him everything she'd discovered, she would see that smoky look come into his eyes, and feel her own body respond with quickening desire. And then he would take her in his arms, and whisper how much he had missed her . . .

But, although the lights were blazing, and the huge front door standing open to welcome her, the great house for once did not exude that magical aura of welcome.

It felt dead, lifeless, just a pile of stone and wood.

For no reason that she could put a finger on, Rio felt all her warm anticipation cool and shrivel in her heart.

She parked the Land Rover, but did not bother to unpack. Instead, she got out, and stretched stiffly on the gravelled drive, looking up at Barramundi with cloudy grey eyes. A figure came hurrying down the staircase to greet her, but it was not Cameron.

It was Joseph, the major-domo. And although he beamed a welcome, spreading his arms wide, his eyes were dark and worried.

'Welcome home, Miss Rio. Your trip was not too taxing?'

'It went well, Joseph.'

Two of the young gardeners had arrived by now. Together, they lifted the luggage out of the Land Rover, and walked back to the house. There was still no sign of Cameron. Then she realised what it was that had disturbed her: his red jeep was missing from its place on the drive.

'Did the man come for the sharks?' she asked Joseph conversationally.

'They took them away on Tuesday, Miss Rio,' he nodded. He volunteered nothing more. But she kept back her questions until they were inside the house, and the rest of the staff were fussing around, directing the various components of Rio's luggage to their varying destinations.

Then she turned to Joseph, and pulled off the scarf she'd worn to cover her hair.

'Where's Cameron, Joseph?'

'Mr Cameron is not here, Miss Rio.' The middle-aged Filipino pretended to be busy with the straps of her suitcase, but she laid her hand gently on his arm.

'Where is he?' she asked quietly, her heart cold and filled with dread inside her.

Joseph straightened, and faced her, and now his eyes were tragic. 'Mr Cameron has gone back to England, Miss Rio. To London.'

'To *London*?' Rio felt the blood turn to ice in her veins 'I don't understand,' she said, shaking her head numbly. 'When did he go?'

'On Monday night.'

'The night after I left?' she asked incredulously.

'Yes.'

'With no—no message—for me?'

Joseph made a little stifled movement, as though he'd wanted to reach out and touch her arm, but had stopped himself in time. 'I'm sorry, Miss Rio,' he said heavily. 'He just said that he would telephone you on Friday night. And goodbye.'

She lay on the bed, listening to the sound of her heart beating in the stillness of the great house. Without Cameron, Barramundi was a vast, empty shell. No life seemed to remain in the high-ceilinged rooms, which now had taken on an echoing, museum-like stillness. Even the staff tiptoed on their errands now, moving with exaggerated care, as though the house had overnight become a house of mourning.

She hadn't slept last night. Lunch and dinner today had

been ghastly affairs, with Rio sitting pale and silent at the huge table, waited on by an absurd number of servants, unable to do more than pick at the meal. She had been all too aware of the downcast eyes, and even worse, of compassionate glances that some had given her. It would have been humiliating if it hadn't been so eerie.

She'd told Joseph that she wouldn't be taking any more meals in the dining-room, that sandwiches in her room would do.

In between, she'd been working on her report with a blind intensity, trying to stop every stray thought that crossed her mind.

Just goodbye.

She knew in her heart what he would say to her when he called on Friday. Why didn't she just pack her bags and depart, tonight, before it happened?

Partly because she wanted to believe, against logic, that there was some other reason for his departure, some crisis at BTS that had called him there. Partly because she was praying that when he called, it would be to ask her to come to him in London.

Partly because, like a hurt animal, she was almost incapable of making any conscious decision yet.

But mostly because leaving Barramundi would be a final acknowledgment that it was all over. For ever.

'Cameron,' she whispered, 'why have you done this to me?'

There was no question that his departure was permanent. According to Joseph, he had driven himself to the private airfield at Musgrave, from where he had taken a Learjet to Darwin to connect with the London flight. He had been landing in London at around the time she was making her last dives on the reef.

Had he thought of her then, when the wheels had touched down at Heathrow? Had he felt guilt, regret, relief?

The bedroom they had shared was devoid of his presence. Most of his clothes were still in the wardrobe. But his intimate possessions weren't there any more. The little silver clock was gone from his side of the bed. The small collection of his toiletries from the bathroom. Extraordinary how much it hurt to see that his toothbrush was missing, his razor, and the bottle of Givenchy aftershave with the painfully haunting smell . . .

The research papers were gone from his desk, which had been tidied completely, and was now as empty as the three pools down there, at the bottom of the garden. Rio's quick eye had even noticed that the fine Burberry overcoat which normally hung on the coat-rack in the study was also gone.

He would need that, of course, to face a London winter.

'Miss Rio?'

She sat up wearily as Joseph came in with a tray of sandwiches. He set them on the bedside table, then switched on the light.

'It is time for your dinner,' he said firmly, anticipating her total lack of appetite. His lined face creased in a smile. 'Eat now, Miss Rio. You need strength.'

'Joseph,' she said quietly, picking up a sandwich to please him, 'has he ever left suddenly, like this before?'

'Well . . .' Joseph was too well trained to shrug. He turned the gesture into a straightening of his white uniform. 'It is not unusual for Mr Cameron to leave Barramundi at short notice. He tends to come and go, so we always keep the house in a state of readiness for him.'

'Is there any chance that he'll come back—I mean soon?'

'I do not think so.' His voice was gentle.

'Joseph, what am I meant to do?' Her eyes pleaded with him for an answer to questions that were too painful to put into words.

He met her eyes, then sat on the bed, a step unusual enough to indicate that he was extremely upset.

'I do not now what you are meant to do, *querida*,'

he said unhappily. 'Just wait for his call. Mr Cameron is not like other men, you know that. He would never hurt deliberately—and never you, Miss Rio, never you.'

'Has this happened before?' She made a little gesture. 'I mean, other women, here at Barramundi. With Cameron.'

'Not like you,' Joseph said decisively. A sad smile crossed his broad face. 'Not like you, Miss Rio. Oh, yes, there have been other women at Barramundi, sometimes big parties of guests, the way it used to be, in the old days. Women have always flocked around Mr Cameron. But there has never been one like you, no woman who meant so much to him. Not here.'

'Not *here*?' she queried, struck by the odd phrase.

'Not at Barramundi.' He hesitated.

'Go on,' she prompted quietly.

'I have been talking to my wife—forgive me, Miss Rio—about you. She said something that seemed wise to me.'

'What was it?'

'She said that Mr Cameron may have gone *because* there has never been anything like you before. That he may have had no other way of parting from you than suddenly, like a surgeon's knife.'

'I don't understand.' Rio stared at him with wide grey eyes. 'You mean he ran away from involvement?'

'Something like that, perhaps.'

Rio shook her head. 'I can't believe that. He was already involved. And he was so . . .' She didn't finish the sentence, but turned to him restlessly. 'Why did he come this time, Joseph? He stayed here for over four months, and I know that his company wanted him back in London. He had already been here too long by the time *I* arrived on the scene. What was the reason he stayed so long?'

Joseph glanced at her with an odd expression, 'Did he not tell you?'

'Tell me what?'

'About what happened in London before he came out

here . . .?' A measure of comprehension dawned across Joseph's dark face. 'He never told you,' he said softly. 'You do not understand.'

'Told me *what*?' Rio asked urgently. Instinctively, she felt she was at last on the threshold of some understanding. She could almost have shaken the major-domo into speaking. 'What happened in London? *Please*, Joseph, I have to know!'

He rubbed his cheek tiredly. 'He came here to get over it. Last year, shortly before he came to Barramundi, Mr Cameron was engaged to be married.'

'Engaged,' she echoed emptily.

'Yes. Engaged to an Englishwoman called Fabia Maxwell.' Joseph's eyes turned in Rio's white face for a moment, as though wondering whether to go on with what he was saying. Rio nodded imperceptibly for him to continue. 'She came to Barramundi once, last year, but that was before the engagement. She was beautiful,' Joseph nodded, 'like you. But taller, and dark. And not so relaxed. Mr Cameron told us that she was the daughter of an English nobleman, and had to be addressed as Lady Fabia.'

'Were they—in love?'

'It did not occur to us then that they might be,' Joseph said frankly. 'It was just a happy party of people, and Lady Fabia was simply one of the guests. The engagement was announced some weeks after they returned to England.'

Rio's voice was dry and papery. 'The wedding. Did it take place?'

'No, Miss Rio, the wedding never took place.' Joseph straightened his uniform again, with that tragic expression back in his dark eyes. 'Lady Fabia died, in London, two months before the wedding.'

'You never told me.' The accusation quivered in the air like a freshly launched arrow. Rio's eyes stared unseeing at the wall ahead of her as she sat on the bed, holding the telephone to her ear. 'All that time, I didn't know.'

'No,' Cameron replied flatly, 'you didn't know.'

'Why did you hide it from me?'

'It was never my intention to hide it, Rio. At first, there was no reason to tell you. We were strangers. And then, suddenly, we were something a lot more intimate. And as we got closer, it became harder and harder to tell you.' His voice, made remote by telephone electronics, drifted on long waves of long-distance static. 'There was a point at which I wanted to tell you, up there on Grey Mare Hill, in the chapel. But somehow I never did. I knew that it would take all the joy out of your eyes, and that made me a coward. And then we were lovers, and I was afraid . . .'

'Afraid that I'd think you were simply consoling yourself with me?' she said.

'Something like that.'

'And is that what you were doing?'

'I was afraid that I might be,' he replied steadily.

'Oh, God,' she whispered in misery. She looked out of the window with blurred eyes. He'd called late, and the moon was already bright in the sky, the silvery moon she'd wished on a few short nights ago . . .

His voice drifted through the static. 'We've never been anything but honest with each other, Rio. Fabia was the only secret I ever had from you, and now I want you to understand everything.' He drew a deep breath. 'I felt that I was your lover under false pretences. If I *was* simply using you to ease my grief, then I had no right to do so. It was criminal. But I couldn't help myself. Things don't always turn out the way we know they ought to, and I didn't want something so beautiful to have an end. You did something to me that was . . . that was very new to me.'

Was. The word struck a leaden note. 'Did you love her?' she asked abruptly.

Cameron hesitated. 'She was very different from you.'

'That's not what I asked, Cameron.' Rio retorted sharply.

He sighed briefly. 'Fabia has been dead for six months, Rio. Are you jealous of a dead woman?'

'Why should I lie, and say I'm not?' Rio demanded fiercely. Her mouth trembled. 'How was she different from me?'

'What happened between you and me was spontaneous, unpremeditated. I believe in fate, Rio, and it was fate that brought us together. Your coming to Australia, the cyclone, the whole unplanned, extraordinary cycle of events—it could never have been anticipated or allowed for.' He paused. 'My relationship with Fabia was not like that. It was something logical, calculated. Our marriage was planned very carefully, with no allowance made for the unexpected. Except the unexpected fact of her death,' he added with the first hint of bitterness he'd shown. 'But it was a relationship that I don't think you could ever understand.'

'You must have loved her,' Rio said tearfully. 'That's all I *do* understand. If you didn't love her, you wouldn't have become engaged to her. And now you've decided that you loved her more than you could ever love me. Isn't that it?'

'No,' he said wearily, 'that isn't it. It isn't a question of comparisons.'

'Then why did you go back to London without me?' It was a cry from the heart, and when he answered her, his voice sounded as though he'd had to harden himself.

'Because it suddenly occurred to me that I couldn't keep on misleading us both, Rio. I've neglected my responsibilities in practically every sense. It was time for me to return to London and face up to the realities of my life.'

'Realities?' she echoed bitterly. 'You mean I've just been a diversion for you?'

'No, that's not what I mean,' he said patiently.

'It hurt so much that you didn't tell me,' she said, her

voice choking. 'When Joseph told me what had happened, I nearly died . . . please wait.' Rio put the phone down and twisted on the bed for a handkerchief to dry her eyes and blow her nose. She would have given anything at that moment to have seen Cameron's face, to have been able to look into those deep blue eyes for understanding. She picked the phone up again, red-eyed. 'Are you still there?'

'Yes,' he said, 'I'm still here.'

She sighed dully. 'Are you calling from your flat?'

'No. I'm in my office, in London. It's mid-morning here. And snowing.'

'I wish I was with you,' she said miserably. 'It's so horribly lonely without you . . .'

'Yes,' he said quietly, 'I know. How was your trip to the cottage?'

'Oh . . .' She sniffed. 'Interesting.'

As though wanting to give her time to pull herself together, he asked her about her findings at the cottage; and for her part, she was glad to have the pretence at normality for a few minutes.

'It's an intriguing conclusion,' he said, when she'd told him how she was going to end her report. 'How much of it is written?'

'Almost all of it.' She'd got her emotions under control now, in a brittle sort of way. 'I've been writing non-stop ever since—ever since I got back.'

'Stay at Barramundi as long as you like,' he urged. 'They'll take care of you. I've left Joseph with full instructions about booking your flights home when you're ready to go. He'll pay all the fares, and take care of all the arrangements.'

'That's very kind of you,' she said, aware of sounding weirdly formal. 'Cameron,' she pleaded, 'what do you want? Is it time you need?'

'Yes, Rio. But I want more than that.'

'You want your freedom from me,' she said heavily.

His voice grew soft. 'You never took my freedom away from me, Rio. You gave me liberty, a liberty which I'd never known before. My life has never been unfettered, not since my childhood. You made me feel, for the first time, that I really could be free. But if I said I simply wanted time, that would imply I was contemplating coming back to you, one day.'

'And you're not?' she asked in a small voice.

'Listen to me,' he said quietly. 'You are a golden girl, Rio. you have so much ahead of you—so much achievement, so much happiness and success. You have a chance to taste freedom, for the first time in your life. It isn't a chance given to many. Take it, and don't look back. Spread your wings and fly, girl. Take whatever life has to offer you, and don't question it.'

'But I love you, Cameron——'

'You love life,' he said tiredly. 'I would chain you to the ground, Rio. I would want to possess you, and maybe never be able to give you anything in return. And you deserve better than that.'

'But I want nothing more than to be possessed by you, for the rest of my life!' Tears were getting in the way again, choking her voice. 'What you call my freedom is just loneliness, Cameron. My life hasn't been free, either. But with you——' She couldn't finish that sentence. 'I would give it up without a second's hesitation if you asked me to.'

His voice was remote again. 'You can't give away anything so precious, Rio.'

'That's what love is!'

'Your love doesn't concern me,' he said harshly. 'Give it to someone else, Rio. Someone who wants it.'

Shock stopped her tears, like a slap across the face. 'Cameron!'

'I mean it, Rio,' he continued grimly. 'Don't waste your love like a fool. I have never wanted it.'

She sat in stunned silence, her throat aching with unshed

tears. A vision of the past weeks flitted through her mind, like a spool of tape being erased. When she spoke at last, her voice was empty and cold, 'Then there's nothing more to be said, is there?'

'Not on that topic,' he agreed briefly. 'But there are other topics. When you get back to London, I want you to get in touch with Alison Williams, my chief personnel officer, at the BTS offices.'

A humourless smile crossed her mouth. 'You're offering me a job?'

'There's a job for you, yes—if you want it. But BTS is offering it, not me.'

She swallowed painfully, adjusting to the businesslike tone he'd adopted. 'Would I—would I be working near you?'

'You'll be working in California, for our American subsidiary. You'll get a salary commensurate with your talent, and a company house and car in San Francisco. The work is mainly concerned with solar heating systems——'

'No, thank you, Cameron,' she said with a weary laugh. 'Either you take responsibility for the whole of me, or not at all. It sounds a lovely job, but I don't want it. Not if the price is giving you up for ever.'

'There's no price,' he said crisply. 'You have considerable talent, Rio, and it's going to be in demand when your report is published. I'm simply trying to secure that talent for my own company.'

'Thanks. But no thanks.'

She half expected him to try and persuade her, but after a short silence he simply said, 'You can always contact me at BTS, Rio. About anything. Any problem you have.'

'Except the problem that I love you.'

'I must go, Rio.' Now his tone was coldly professional, like an authoritative stranger's. 'I have a board meeting in ten minutes.'

'I can't believe that this is happening,' she said dully. 'I can't believe that this is you talking . . .'

'I must go,' he repeated, his voice oddly dry as he cut her trembling sentence through. 'Take care. Goodbye, Rio.'

CHAPTER TEN

THE wave generator had been working for the past three days now, slooshing the sea-water in the giant tank to and fro, despite the fact that only a handful of specimens were already installed. Rio had programmed the Aqua-Master microprocessor, which would eventually control all the systems in the tank automatically, to adjust the impulses continuously. The water surged to a realistic, irregular rhythm, and it was odd how exactly, in the echoing chamber, it matched the real sound of the ocean.

If she were to shut her eyes now, and concentrate on the heat bathing her skin, the smell of the salt air, and that ceaseless, primordial rhythm, she could really imagine herself on the beach, back at Barramundi . . .

Except that the heat was generated by the extensive bank of sun-lamps above the tank, and Liverpool was on the other side of the world from Barramundi.

'Rio?'

She opened her eyes. Malcolm Ellison, the co-ordinator of the project, was waving urgently to her from the gallery. 'The Australian Consulate is on the line.'

'Coming.'

She clambered gingerly along the scaffolding, clad in denim jeans and a black sweater, lowered herself into the gallery, and ran to the telephone in the Aquarium Management suite.

The call was from the extraordinarily helpful attaché whom they'd already had several meetings with, and who'd singlehandedly cut more red tape than Rio had dared hope. 'Your specimens have arrived, Miss Faber,' he told her, sounding quite excited. 'They're waiting on the docks, here in Liverpool. You can pick them up this afternoon, as soon as Customs have released them.'

'I'll arrange to pick them up right away,' Rio said, her heart beating faster with anticipation. 'Can you be on hand this afternoon, Mr Purvis? The Press will want some photographs, I should imagine.'

'No problem,' he assured her.

'Then I'll ring you back as soon as I've got a wagon to pick them up.'

She put the phone down, and turned to Malcolm with shining eyes.

'Well?' he demanded.

'They're here. On the docks!'

'Bingo!' He gave her a quick hug. It was one of the moments they'd been waiting and planning for ever since the project had been initiated. From now on, the planning and preparation were over—and the real work of fitting out the Coral Tank had begun.

'I'll get a container wagon organised,' Malcom said briskly, moving to the telephone. 'Lizzie can handle the Press. And we'll need a lot of extra staff this afternoon. Do you want to do any last-minute checks on the Tank?'

'Yes,' Rio nodded, 'I think I'd better. I didn't expect them to arrive so soon. See you at lunch?'

She walked quickly back to the Coral Tank. This time, instead of going in through the back door, high up at the back of the tank, she went in through the main entrance, the way the public would come in when the tank was opened.

'Tank' was an almost insulting word to describe what she and Malcolm, and their team, had created here over the past weeks. It was, in the truest sense, a replica of a marine environment. An artificial eco-system, complete with rock, sand, and constantly moving water, bathed in electric sunlight.

When Malcolm had asked her to help set the project up, soon after her return from Australia, she'd known immediately that the Coral Tank would be one of the most revolutionary developments in aquarium technology. A large-scale system, containing over a hundred and fifty animal and plant species from the Great Barrier Reef. A display that would give visitors a real idea—through glass—of what it was like to dive on a coral reef; and that was utterly different from anything that had been tried in a British aquarium before.

She stared at the scene. It really was like something from the Barrier Reef. The tank they'd created held three thousand gallons of sea-water. The salinity and oxygen levels were very carefully monitored, and in the end would be controlled by the same computer program which would also control the banks of sun-lamps overhead, the induction heaters which kept the water tropically warm, and the supply of food.

'It's going to be absolutely beautiful,' one of the kids said, excitedly. 'Today's the big day, Rio!'

'Yes,' she agreed gently. 'Today's the big day.' It hadn't escaped her notice that most of the boys had fallen head over heels in love with her during these past weeks. Her tan had faded to silver-gold through the course of an English winter; but her body was still as exquisitely trim as it had been during those Australian weeks.

High-breasted and long-legged, she moved with a feminine grace that drew male eyes like a magnet; and her face had the perfect beauty of a Botticelli angel. On the days that she dived in the tank, they crowded the railings, forgetting their own jobs, to watch.

Yet the kids' attention gave her no pleasure, not even amusement.

Kids. She'd been a kid herself, like one of these students from the Marine Biology Department of the University, before she'd left for Australia. Now, her experience was a million miles away from theirs, her heart schooled to a harsh reality that was utterly different from the optimistic gaiety she saw in their faces.

In her jeans and sweater, her golden hair fluttering free, you could easily mistake her for one of the students. Until you looked into those beautiful grey eyes, and saw the maturity there.

She moved along the gallery. What would she have done without this project to keep herself from falling apart?

God knew. She'd returned from Barramundi with the sense that a phase in her life had come to an end, that a door had closed behind her for ever, leaving her exposed, out in the cold. When she'd completed her paper, and had sent it off for publication, she'd realised that she was more desperately lonely and confused than at any time since her parents had died.

But for Malcolm Ellison and the Coral Tank, her long ride back to emotional stability would have been agonisingly rocky. As it was, he'd been impatiently awaiting her return to speak to her about the project. He'd been a postgraduate research fellow during her Oxford years, before joining the Aquarium in Liverpool, and he'd seen her as the ideal person to set the Coral Tank up in Liverpool.

He'd come down to see her at the Foundation's offices with little more than a handful of notes to explain what he wanted her to do.

'I know you'll want to start looking around for a job,' he pleaded, 'but this will only take a few months, and although the pay won't be brilliant, the experience might be valuable.'

And she'd accepted the offer like a drowning person clutching at a lifebelt. Malcolm had never known how much this job had meant to her. He'd taken her almost feverishly intense involvement for granted, never suspecting that she was using the project to displace pain, never realising that she was using it to hold herself together.

But that was exactly what she'd been doing. Consciously surrounding herself with calm. Keeping herself cocooned within her work, barely noticing that anything else existed outside of it.

The Tank was almost finished. Soon, she was going to have to look for a real job. At least, though, she now had the inner strength and self-control to face the task. For now, the Tank was all that mattered.

Rio had no illusions that she had loved, and lost. No man would ever take the place of Cameron in her heart, not now, not in the future.

No man's love would ever touch her in the way he'd touched her. In the way he would always, until her dying day, touch her.

She didn't have to make any resolutions about not thinking of Cameron. Cameron was deep inside her, would always be a part of her. Memories of him came and went across the stage of her consciousness, unbidden, but always adored.

Sometimes, too, there had been a feeling of closeness to him that was totally eerie.

On at least two occasions, when she'd been working on the tank, under the blaze of the sun-lamps, the strangest feeling had come over her that Cameron was watching her, from the dark gallery beyond. A feeling so strong that she could have sworn she could even make out his tall figure in the inky blackness. A feeling that had flooded her skin with white heat. Until she couldn't bear it any more.

And each time, when she'd climbed over the rail, her heart pounding with excitement, and had moved out of the blinding light, the gallery had been empty.

She'd been pierced by a sense of disappointment that had

shattered her calm, and made her curse her own vivid imagination.

Through it all, that starlit realisation had remained, guiding her through the darkness—that without him, her life would have been immeasurably poorer.

Tanya Wilkins, wearing full scuba gear and one of the Aquarium's yellow wet-suits, had been drifting along the bottom of the tank, checking the inlets. Now she glanced at Rio through the plate-glass wall, waved, and kicked up to the surface.

Dripping, she hauled herself up the aluminium rungs, pulling her mask back. 'All systems go down here,' she spluttered, clinging to the top rung. 'I hear the Australian specimens have arrived?'

'Yes.' Rio shook herself out of her reverie. 'They're here.' As if the urgency of the situation had just started to dawn on her, Rio went on, 'Listen, Tanya, since you're wet, will you take water samples and get them to the Lab? Ask them to run a spot check for any sort of pollution, please. I want everything to be absolutely perfect for this afternoon.'

She passed Tanya two of the little brown bottles they used for sampling, then hurried to the little control-room to check the mainline systems.

She had to try and anticipate any possible disaster that might kill the corals that would be installed this afternoon. They had come from so far, with the help and good will of so many people—especially the Australian government, who had supervised the removal and export of most of the specimens for this Tank.

Everything seemed under control. All the dials were reading normal levels.

Simulating the wave action of the sea was going to be one of the key factors to keeping the coral reef healthy. The lights, and careful monitoring of the water, would help to simulate the natural conditions of the Great Barrier Reef. Already, their modest collection of corals and reef fauna appeared to be thriving, though it remained to be seen whether the tank could sustain the really large population that she and Malcolm had envisaged for it—for it was the size and scale of the Coral Tank that made it so unique.

She'd never quite got over the irony that the Aqua-Master control-board was a Biotechnology Systems product, supplied to aquariums and big fish-tanks across Europe.

The BTS logo drew her eyes now, triggering a concentrated rush of memory that was like the release of some fierce drug in her bloodstream.

She closed her eyes over the precious memory that filled her mind, like the scent of crushed herbs. It was so often the same memory, of that last night they'd spent together at Barramundi, of the candle-light playing across their naked bodies, of the love they'd made . . .

'I've got us a couple of salad rolls from the cafeteria.' Oblivious to her dizzy mood, Malcolm hustled into the little room on a wave of raw onions and enthusiasm. 'We'll just gobble it down and get across to the docks, what do you say?'

With a supreme effort, Rio dragged herself into the present . 'OK,' she said, accepting the food she didn't really want. 'I suppose it's going to be a long day.'

A fortnight later, the Australian Consul held a reception for them.

By that time, it had become abundantly clear to even the most sceptical observers that the Coral Tank was a stunning success, and on the morning of the reception, Rio and Malcolm had entertained delegations from two of the biggest British aquariums, who had come to inspect the venture with unfeigned admiration.

The spectacular beauty of the new Coral Tank had also been featured on local television, on the national network, on Children's TV, and in at least a dozen newspaper and magazine articles. And the public had been queuing three deep every day to get into the Aquarium.

The mood at the reception, consequently, was jubilant. It was held at the Consulate, an imposing Georgian building with a fine view of the port, and champagne and congratulations were the order of the evening.

'Which isn't the end of her talents,' a beaming Malcolm Ellison was assuring their host and hostess, and the principal guests. 'She's just had an article published in *New Scientist*.'

'Really?' The consul's wife looked suitably impressed. 'What about?'

'It's really no more than a few thoughts I had,' Rio smiled, playing it down. The pale green silk dress was new, and very flattering. It made a classically perfect foil for her tanned skin and golden hair, and warmed the cool shade of her grey eyes. In the circle of dark-suited men, she looked like a tropical flower. 'No more than the main points of the paper I delivered to the Foundation.'

'Rio recently did some important research on the Great Barrier Reef for the Cotton Foundation,' the Consul explained to the listening circle. 'Malcolm couldn't have found anyone more perfect to set up the Coral Tank.'

'Rio's a very bright lady,' Malcolm assured them all, making Rio cringe inside with embarrassment. Being the centre of attention wasn't altogether pleasant. She wanted to enjoy the evening, partly because this party was going to mark the end of the Coral project. There was really nothing left for her to do at the Aquarium; from now on, she was back on her own . . .

'Well, I'm grateful to Miss Faber from a purely selfish point of view.' The man who was 'something in local politics' toasted Rio with his champagne glass. 'It's nice to see Liverpool in the news about something other than inner city blight or football hooliganism.'

'I love Liverpool,' Rio smiled at him. 'It's a very great city.'

For a while the talk was of regional triumphs and disasters, mercifully taking the limelight off Rio, until the Consul's wife shepherded them towards the buffet table.

'I don't want anybody to be shy,' she urged, loading Rio's plate with smoked salmon and dressed crab hors-d'oeuvres. 'this is an occasion for a feast.'

As soon as she could, Rio surreptitiously exchanged the plate for a selection of things that looked as though they might be mainly vegetable in origin. Since Barramundi, she'd stopped making any kind of fuss about her vegetarianism, but whenever she could she stuck to a non-meat diet. Amused irony creased her mouth as she thought of those marvellous steaks on the beach, when the world was tearing itself apart all around them ...

The party was filling rapidly, to the point where it was no longer practical for Rio to be introduced to every new arrival.

Instead, as the centre of attention—and, incidentally, by far the prettiest woman in the room—she found herself being passed from group to eager group. Rather like a rugby ball, she thought with an inner smile, though the handling was a great deal gentler.

Through the row of tall Georgian windows, the lights of the harbour were glittering in the cold, clear night outside. Inside, cheeks were growing flushed, and the happy noise was reaching the stage when you had to strain to hear what someone next to you was saying. It was easier to just let snatches of conversations around her drift into her ears.

'So I said, "It may be a passable *imitation* of Chanel, dear, but *nothing* beats the real thing, does it?"'

'Edward's been in London on one of his boring Quangos all this week, so I've had the bedroom done out in French blue ...'

'She had a lovely figure, but plump, you know, puppy fat

you would call it really, but you could tell she would run to doggy fat in a couple of years if she didn't watch her diet . . .'

'If the export situation doesn't get any better this year, we're seriously going to consider Taiwan . . .'

'She didn't! She couldn't have! I refuse to believe it, Hugo!'

'And then the silly fool went and changed parties, and promptly lost his deposit at the next election . . .'

Rio smiled inwardly. Thank goodness everyone had stopped talking about the Coral Tank, and how wonderful Rio Faber was. She found that she was staring absently across the room at a male back. There was suddenly something so painfully familiar about that back that her heart had started pounding.

The same broad shoulders and commanding height, and though the black-air was closer cropped than Cameron's had ever been, this man might almost have been Cameron.

He was talking to the Consul's wife, and she watched him make a gesture that she thought she recognised. Rio suddenly had an urgent need to see his face. Of course it couldn't be. It was impossible. But what if——

Excusing herself abruptly, she edged through the crowd with her heart in her throat, straining to catch a glimpse of the man's profile. Insane to raise her hopes like this. But what if? Could it possibly be——? With a surge of excitement, she felt that she was right, it *was* Cameron! A smile of pure joy lit up her face as she squeezed between two groups of people to get closer and put her arms round him——

Abruptly, he turned and stared across the room in her direction.

Disappointment was an almost physical pain that lanced through her. This man had a thin, moustached, unintelligent face, not remotely like Cameron's. She felt all her muscles sag in anticlimax, and for a moment, she squeezed her temples between the thumb and forefinger of her left hand, aware of a growing headache that probably wouldn't go away tonight.

This was just like those weird occasions at the Aquarium, when she'd been convinced that Cameron was out there, just beyond the dazzling lights ... When was she going to learn?

Fool. She'd just ruined a perfectly pleasant evening for herself. Right now, she just felt like going straight back to her digs and crying on her bed. Oh, you pathetic *fool* ...

She was barely aware of the kindly hand that took her arm, except to feel an inner revulsion at having to continue the sociable charade any longer. She *wasn't* happy, she *wasn't* in the mood for any damned party, and——

'That's Simon Kennedy,' the quiet, deep voice informed her. He's a rising magazine publisher.' Stunned, Rio turned to face Cameron Frazer.

The *real* Cameron Frazer.

He tilted a dark eyebrow at her. 'Did you think he was me?' he asked calmly.

She nodded slightly, still speechless with disbelief.

'I saw it in your face.' His eyes were deep blue as the sea, deep enough to drown in. He surveyed her with a faint smile. 'You've never been able to hide your feelings, Rio. Has anyone told you it's a fault?'

'Oh, Cameron,' she choked, dizziness washing over her like a wave.

'Behave,' he growled, stopping her from melting into his arms with a warning frown. 'We're in public.'

'What are you *doing* here?' she asked faintly, her throat almost too dry to form the sound. He looked utterly magnificent in evening dress. No matter how faithful her memory was, it could never have recalled his sheer presence, the way he towered head and shoulders above other men. Her heart was fluttering like a trapped bird. 'I feel as though I must be dreaming!'

'I know most of the Australian diplomatic community,' he said. 'It wasn't hard to wangle an invitation.' His once-unruly hair, black as a raven's wing, had been cut in Curzon Street since she'd last seen him. It gave him a formidable air of sophistication, but his dark tan still gave those piercing blue eyes that heart-stopping emphasis. They were focused on her now with almost brooding intensity. 'You've been achieving great things,' he murmured. 'What do you plan for an encore?'

Suddenly, she badly needed to sit down.

'It's been horrible without you,' she said helplessly. It was a torment to have him so close to her, and not to be able to touch him the way she wanted to. A little colour had returned to her cheeks now, and the steel fist around her heart had started releasing its grip. She held her champagne glass in trembling hands, and smiled unsteadily up at him. 'You look marvellous, Cameron.'

'And you look like a rose,' he replied softly. Someone had approached them from the side, and was trying to edge into the conversation, but they ignored him so completely that he faded back into the crowd with a shrug. It was obvious that this man and woman had eyes only for one another.

'Every time I pick up the paper, I seem to find myself reading about you,' Cameron said. 'You've become the darling of the hour.'

'It'll only be an hour,' she smiled wryly. Cameron hadn't been out of her mind for a single day of the past three months, yet the impact of seeing him here was like that first shock of seeing him on the beach, aeons ago. 'I'm beginning to wonder if I haven't over-specialised. There can't be that many jobs for an expert on corals . . .'

'You won't even have to go looking.' Cameron lifted a champagne glass from a passing waiter's tray. 'You're going to be offered contracts by at least two big chemical firms shortly. No,' he added drily as he saw her expression, 'I assure you that BTS isn't behind them. They're real enough.' He saluted her with the glass, and drank.

'It's nice to know you're wanted,' she said with faint irony. She looked up into the brilliant depths of those magnificent blue eyes. 'How have you been, Cameron?'

'Busy,' he shrugged. 'There was a mountain of work waiting for me when I got back.'

'I told you you'd been playing truant,' she reminded him. Studying him more closely, she saw that the relaxation of Barramundi was gone from his face. The harsh lines of his cheekbones were tauter than she remembered, the expression of his eyes grimmer. It made him look even more ruthlessly handsome than ever. 'I think you've been working too hard,' she informed him.

'I might say the same about you,' he commented. His eyes drifted up and down her slender figure. 'Though it seems to suit you. When I saw you across the room tonight, you struck me as more beautiful than I've ever seen you.'

'Thank you sir,' she said. Rio fiddled with her glass, her face slightly flushed. 'I didn't think I'd ever see you again, Cameron.'

He didn't answer that directly, but smiled slightly. 'Sometimes we do crazy things, thinking them deeply wise.'

'Have you ever——' She hesitated over the painful question, then went ahead with it. 'Have you ever questioned whether you were right to leave me?'

'Yes, I've questioned it,' he nodded, his expression more sombre. 'And I've questioned whether I should have told you more, tried to explain more.'

'Then you do think of me?' Rio asked him, her eyes as soft as mist.

'I've never stopped thinking about you.' He smiled, his mouth all passionate male sensuality. 'I was right, that night at the cottage. You do haunt me, Rio. You'll haunt me for the rest of my life.'

She searched his face urgently, her heart tight in her throat. 'Are you going to go away again, Cameron?'

His voice was husky. 'Do you want me to?'

'Not ever,' she whispered. 'Oh, my love—I know you must have cared very deeply for Fabia, but that was something I could have lived with——'

'Ah!' The Consul's wife had arrived, beaming, and to Rio's unutterable frustration she interposed herself between them. 'I see you two have met already,' she carolled. 'Mr Frazer was *very* keen to meet you, Rio. He's come all the way up from London tonight—and you'll have so much in common. *So* much. I take it you've introduced yourselves already——?'

'We know each other well,' Rio nodded, just wanting to be left alone with Cameron.

'You *naughty* man,' their hostess chided Cameron. 'I thought you just wanted an introduction, when it was really a *reunion* you were after!' She turned her smile on to Rio. 'We're all terribly proud of Cameron, you know. He's a living embodiment of British-Australian achievement——'

Rio listened tautly to the rush of well meaning *bonhomie*. By now, she'd realised that the Consul's wife thought Cameron had come here tonight to offer her a job with BTS. Amusing at any other time, but right now it was all irrelevant to her. Next to the tall dark man who stood smiling faintly at her, next to the conversation that had just been interrupted, nothing in the world had any relevance at all.

And, to her horror, a group of people had started to form around them. They weren't going to have any privacy at all. Anguish filled the glance she shot Cameron, but he merely shook his head imperceptibly, his smile telling her to be patient, and wait.

'I bought two hundred BTS shares eighteen months ago,' someone was saying loudly, 'and they were the best investment I've ever made.'

She let the talk wash over her, unable to take her eyes off

Cameron. Her mouth was dry, her knees weak as water. Above all, one thing remained in her whirling mind. He'd come to find her. He was here, in Liverpool, smiling beautifully at strangers, his eyes always returning to her with that secret inner glint.

She rubbed her bare arms, feeling every inch of her fine skin alive with goose-flesh. The old, old ache of desire was throbbing in her, a hunger that only Cameron could ever fill. *Play it cool*, she warned herself desperately. Hide the way you feel about him. You've had enough practise!

But there was a joy in her heart, making it soar like a lark, that had been dead since she'd left Barramundi . . .

The party seemed to go on for ever. No sooner had one group started to break up, then another one was already starting to cluster. And if she herself was not the centre of conversation, then it was Cameron on whom all eyes were turned. It wasn't until midnight had been passed that Malcolm Ellison finally came to her rescue.

'Rio looks exhausted,' he said firmly. 'She's been working like a Trojan every day for the past three and half months, and it's time she got a rest.'

'I'll give you a lift home,' Cameron had materialised magically at her side again, and was smiling down at her. 'My car's just downstairs. If you'd like that?'

It was very hard not to let out her vast sigh of relief. 'Yes, please,' she said softly. 'I'd like that very much.'

In the leather-and-walnut-trimmed Jaguar, he turned to her with a smile. 'I thought that was going to go on for ever.'

'So did I,' she said with a shuddering sigh, leaning back.

He touched her cheek with warm fingers. 'I'm staying at the Hilton,' he told her, 'in town. Shall we go and talk there?'

'Yes,' she nodded, and he eased the big car out of the quiet street.

His suite at the Hilton, predictably, was huge. Her feet sank into the carpet as he led her through, and made her sit on the wide, white leather sofa that faced the balcony.

He mixed drinks at the black-lacquered cabinet, then came to sit beside her, loosening his tie. '*Prosit.*'

'Mud in your eye.' She sipped the martini, then giggled, 'this has a very naughty feel about it, Cameron—glamorous, but naughty.'

His eyes weren't smiling. 'Do you know why I came to Liverpool today?' he asked gently.

'I hoped—I hoped it was to see me.'

He leaned back, cradling his glass in strong, tanned hands. 'Back there, at the Consulate, you said that you could accept my love for Fabia.'

'I meant it,' she nodded, grey eyes watching his face carefully.

He turned to her with a wry expression. 'Could you accept the fact that I *didn't* love her?'

She was lost for words momentarily. 'I don't understand what you mean,' she said quietly.

'I mean exactly what I say.' Restlessly, he put the glass down, and swung to face her intently. 'I never loved Fabia Maxwell,' he said brusquely. 'I told you that it was a marriage that was very carefully planned, Rio, and I wasn't exaggerating. The only difference between us was that Fabia felt rather more than I did. At the end, I think she may even have loved me. But I was no more than fond of her. Not at any time.'

She stared at him with wide eyes, her whole image of the engagement changing. 'Then why——?'

'Sir Michael Maxwell is chairman of Maxwell Chemicals,' he said with brutal frankness. 'And he had no other children, in particular, no son. My marriage to Fabia was going to mean an amalgamation of the two companies, to form a super-company called Frazer-Maxwell, which I would in time come to own completely. I had wealth, and

BTS. Fabia had an aristrocratic name, and Maxwell Chemicals.' His face grew bitter. 'It was a marriage made in heaven.'

'Don't sound so cynical,' she said quietly, touching his hand. 'Millions of marriages are based on far shakier grounds than those, Cameron.'

'Oh, the ground was rock-solid,' he nodded, his smile dry as wine vinegar. 'The only thing that was missing was love. I'd tried to fight down my feelings of guilt and revulsion at what I was doing, Rio, but they were still there. I knew perfectly well that my motive in marrying was little more than ambition. Naked, thrusting ambition. I already had so much. With Maxwell Chemicals in the basket, I would have saved myself twenty more years of effort. I would have made it to the top—the *real* top—by a single move.'

Rio moved slightly against the smooth leather. 'But she was beautiful, too . . .'

'She was beautiful,' Cameron nodded, and answered the unspoken question with a quick shake of his head. 'No, my love. There wasn't even that to hold us together. Sexually, she meant nothing to me. She was just a means to an end.'

'And Fabia?' Rio asked quietly. 'Didn't she see *you* as just a means to an end?'

'Not in such a ruthless way.' His eyes were sad. 'She told me that all she wanted from me was my children. She was the sort of woman to whom having a family was going to be the focus of her life.'

'She sounds rather nice,' Rio said painfully, putting down the drink she didn't want any more, and folding her hands in her lap.

'She *was* nice,' Cameron nodded. 'But I wasn't.' He stared out of the window, at the diamond lights of the city, then sighed heavily. 'The past five years had been a very hard battle to push BTS to the top. I'd been obsessed with success and achievement for so long that I'd lost any sense of proportion I might have had. Nothing seemed to matter to me except getting ahead. I'd begun to feel that money and power were the most important things in life. That everything should be subservient to those goals, even love itself. I was losing my humanity, Rio.' He glanced at her pale face with dark eyes. 'It took Fabia's illness to bring all that home to me.'

'Did you know it was going to be fatal?' she asked.

'Yes,' he said heavily, 'we all knew. When it was diagnosed, the doctors gave her two months to live. In the event, she only lived for six weeks.'

There was nothing she could say but the old, old words. 'I'm sorry, Cameron.'

'She died peacefully, and without pain. If I'd loved her,' he said quietly, holding her eyes, 'it might have been easier to accept. But it all seemed to crash down on me like a load of bricks—all the guilt and self-blame that I'd refused to acknowledge. It was as though we were being rebuked for cold-heartedness, or ambition, or whatever you like to call it. It was like a punishment.'

'No!' Urgently, she took his hands. 'It wasn't your fault! It wasn't anybody's fault.'

He smiled drily. 'It's taken me half a year to reach that level of understanding, Rio. I'm not gifted with your clear-sightedness.'

'And that was the real reason you went back to Barramundi?'

'Yes. After Fabia died, my life went through a crisis that had been building up for a long time. I knew that I needed to disengage myself completely from my London life, and get back to my roots. Back to nature, for want of a better word. The sharks,' he smiled, 'were the result of a request that a big diving company made to me a couple of months earlier. But the real reason for going back was to teach myself that there was a great deal more to life than money and success.'

'You should have told me all this, long ago,' she said,

stroking his hands. 'You had no right to keep it to yourself. I'd have understood.'

'Would you?' He lifted her hands, and kissed them tenderly. 'I found more than myself at Barramundi, Rio. The day I first saw you, walking naked up the beach, I knew that my life had changed for ever. I knew in my heart that I had finally found what was real in life. It was as though you were a living embodiment of everything that had been missing in my life. As though you were the other half I was born to find.' His lips were warm against the cold skin of her hands. 'And what subsequently happened between us was the most wonderful thing I've ever experienced. For the first time in my life, I knew that I was in love.'

'Then why did you go?' she asked in a whisper.

'Because I had a sudden moment of terror. I told you that I believed in fate? It seemed to me then, as it still seems now, that I didn't deserve you, my love. That you'd be taken away from me, like Fabia, as a punishment for the sin of arrogance.'

'Oh, Cameron!' she gasped, but he touched her lips to silence her.

'We all do and think crazy things, especially when we're in love. I was terrified by the thought that I might be responsible for your coming to harm.'

'But *why*?'

'Would you believe me if I said it was for your sake, Rio?' He smiled wryly. 'I still wasn't sure I'd got my ruthless side under proper control. I'd gone to Barramundi to get my sense of values into perspective again, because I didn't want to keep on living as the man I'd turned into—a man to whom money and prestige mattered more than any human value.'

'You could never be like that,' she said quietly. 'I've known for a long time that you're a man who was born to achieve great things. And I can believe that your values may have been distorted for a while—but you just aren't capable of that sort of life, Cameron. You're too real. I've never met anyone that I could respect as much as I do you.'

'But I had to be sure that I'd really left that madness behind me, Rio. I had to accept my own humanity, not reject it.'

'Frazer's Law,' she smiled.

'Yes,' he nodded. 'Frazer's Law. And if I hadn't found my manhood, then I had no right to you. And I had a terrible premonition that if I hadn't really changed inside, the same thing would happen all over again. I needed to test myself, to test my love for you.' His eyes were almost black as he looked at her. 'And I couldn't go on living without you, Rio. Losing you would have destroyed me.'

'You never have to lose me again.'

'I never want to. Leaving Barramundi was the hardest thing I've ever done. It tore me apart to think of your suffering. I knew it would hit you even harder, because it would come as more of a shock to you. But it was something I simply had to do.' He glanced at her with a smile in his eyes. 'Not that I lost touch with you. I've been following you every inch of the way. I always knew where you were, and what you were doing. A couple of times, when I couldn't stand being separated from you any longer, I used to fly up here, and come to the Aquarium, I used to let myself in by the side door, and watch you from the gallery.'

'Then it *was* you,' she whispered. 'You were there, after all?'

'Yes,' he said softly, 'I was there, watching you. Loving you. I think those were the most painful moments of all, little one, when I could feast my eyes on you, but couldn't come down and touch you, the way I wanted to . . .'

'I knew it was you,' she said, her eyes blurring with tears. 'But every time I came to look, you were gone.'

'At the end, I was utterly sure. Sure of you, sure of myself. But, by then, you'd reached the peak of your work here, and I had to endure just a little more sweet agony until you were done.' He laughed softly. 'Your triumph gave me so much pleasure, Rio. That Coral Tank is all you—exquisitely, ravishingly beautiful, like nothing else on earth. It shows how much talent and creativity is in you. It was worth waiting, to see what you could achieve.'

She looked down, overcome by his praise, then glanced up at his face again. 'Why did you come here tonight?'

'To ask you to forgive me,' he said quietly. 'I've been cruel to you, Rio, and I've hurt you more than I ever had a right to.'

'If there was anything to forgive,' she smiled, 'then it was forgiven right from the start. You don't have to ask for that, Cameron.'

He drew a deep breath, as though a heavy weight had been lifted off his shoulders. 'Thank you, Rio,' he said quietly. His expression was still tense. 'I came for another reason. To ask you to marry me.'

'Oh, my love!' she choked, tears spilling over her lids. 'Why did you take so long?'

His arms were so strong, cradling her the way they'd done so long ago, when a cyclone had raged over their heads. Sobbing, Rio clung to him, her emotions experiencing a release that she'd dreamed of so often over the past winter. His body was wonderfully comforting and warm, his strength marvellous around her weakness.

'My darling,' he said shakily, 'you've just made me so very happy . . .'

'I thought I was going to die without you, Cameron,' she choked.

He cupped her face in his hands, whispering her name. And as her mouth opened to the domination of his kiss, the wonder of him filled her, like the rising sun. After so many lonely, cold, empty days, she felt her life flood with joy again.

'Are you sure this time?' she asked him, looking up with

adoration into the face that had haunted her dreams for so long. 'No reservations, no forebodings?'

'None. I saw the disappointment on your face tonight, when you realised that Simon Kennedy wasn't me. I realised then that you felt exactly the way I did—that we belonged together. For ever.' He touched her lips wonderingly. 'You're so very beautiful, Rio. More beautiful than any dream ...'

'No more dreams,' she promised. 'This is the reality. You've come for me, the way I always knew you would. From now on, my love, we'll always be together ...'

'Always,' he repeated softly, his mouth buried in the fragrant silk of her hair. 'I love you, Rio. God knows how I ever thought I could survive without you by my side. The past three months have been hell.'

'But they've taken away any doubts.' She smiled tremulously. 'Maybe we both needed that period of testing, just to make sure. At least we both know what we feel now. There'll never be any more doubts between us.' She took his tanned face in her hands, looking into his eyes. 'I love you, Cameron.'

'And I love you. I have always loved you.'

'Could you really put up with a vegetarian wife?' she smiled tenderly.

'To the last carrot,' he vowed. 'Could you put up with a husband who insisted you worked for his company?'

'Dear me,' she sighed in mock-disappointment. 'And I was so looking forward to a life of sun, sex and idleness ...'

'You can have all of the first two you want,' he smiled. 'But as for the third—uh-uh. I have far too much respect for your brains to let them moulder. Oh, Rio, there's so much for you to do at BTS, so much we can do together, so much we can achieve ...'

She surrendered her mouth to his kiss, loving him with every fibre of her being.

'I want us to marry in London,' he laughed huskily,

drawing back. 'As soon as decently possible. Then we'll spend our honemoon on the yacht, cruising in the Coral Sea. Do you approve?'

'I approve,' she nodded solemnly. 'I have very fond memories of that yacht.'

'Right now,' he laughed huskily, 'I want you so badly that it hurts.'

'Then make love to me,' she whispered, shameless in her love for him. 'Make it all up to me, now, tonight, for all the nights we've missed . . .'

And as he picked her up in his arms, and carried her effortlessly to the bed, she knew that her life with Cameron was going to be alive with magic and laughter; a life that was going to be filled with more love and joy than she had ever dared to dream of.

ATTRACTIVE, SPACE SAVING BOOK RACK

Display your most prized novels on this handsome and sturdy book rack. The hand-rubbed walnut finish will blend into your library decor with quiet elegance, providing a practical organizer for your favorite hard-or soft-covered books.

Only $9.95

Approximately 16" x 8" when assembled

Assembles in seconds!

To order, rush your name, address and zip code, along with a check or money order for $10.70* ($9.95 plus 75¢ postage and handling) payable to *Harlequin Reader Service*:

Harlequin Reader Service
Book Rack Offer
901 Fuhrmann Blvd.
P.O. Box 1396
Buffalo, NY 14269-1396

Offer not available in Canada.

BKR-1A

*New York and Iowa residents add appropriate sales tax.

*Exciting, adventurous, sensual stories
of love long ago*

On Sale Now:

SATAN'S ANGEL by Kristin James

*Slater was the law in a land that was as wild and untamed
as he was himself, but all that changed when he met
Victoria Stafford. She had been raised to be a lady, but
that didn't mean she had no will of her own. Their search
for her kidnapped cousin brought them together, but they
were too much alike for the course of true love to run
smooth.*

PRIVATE TREATY by Kathleen Eagle

*When Jacob Black Hawk rescued schoolteacher
Carolina Hammond from a furious thunderstorm, he
swept her off her feet in every sense of the word, and she
knew that he was the only man who would ever make her
feel that way. But society had put barriers between them
that only the most powerful and overwhelming love could
overcome . . .*

Look for them wherever Harlequin books are sold.   HIS-CNM-1

Temptation™

TEMPTATION WILL BE
EVEN HARDER TO RESIST...

In September, Temptation is presenting a sophisticated new
face to the world. A fresh look that truly brings Harlequin's
most intimate romances into focus.

What's more, all-time favorite authors Barbara Delinsky, Rita
Clay Estrada, Jayne Ann Krentz and Vicki Lewis Thompson
will join forces to help us celebrate. The result? A very special
quartet of Temptations...

- **Four striking covers**
- **Four stellar authors**
- **Four sensual love stories**
- **Four variations on one spellbinding theme**

All in one great month! Give in to Temptation in September.

TDESIGN-1

Coming in April
Harlequin Category Romance Specials!

Look for six new and exciting titles from this mix of two genres.

4 Regencies—lighthearted romances set in England's Regency period (1811-1820)

2 Gothics—romance plus suspense, drama and adventure

Regencies

Daughters Four by Dixie Lee McKeone
She set out to matchmake for her sister, but reckoned without the Earl of Beresford's devilish sense of humor.

Contrary Lovers by Clarice Peters
A secret marriage contract bound her to the most interfering man she'd ever met!

Miss Dalrymple's Virtue by Margaret Westhaven
She needed a wealthy patron—and set out to buy one with the only thing she had of value....

The Parson's Pleasure by Patricia Wynn
Fate was cruel, showing her the ideal man, then making it impossible for her to have him....

Gothics

Shadow over Bright Star by Irene M. Pascoe
Did he want her shares to the silver mine, her love—or her life?

Secret at Orient Point by Patricia Werner
They seemed destined for tragedy despite the attraction between them....

CAT88A-1

Lynda Ward's

LEAP THE MOON

...the continuing saga of *The Welles Family*

You've already met Elaine Welles, the oldest daughter of powerful tycoon Burton Welles, in Superromance #317, *Race the Sun*. You cheered her on as she threw off the shackles of her heritage and won the love of her life, Ruy de Areias.

Now it's her sister's turn. Jennie Welles is the drop-dead-gorgeous, most rebellious Welles sister, and she's determined to live life her way—and flaunt it in her father's face.

When she meets Griffin Stark, however, she learns there's more to life than glamour and independence. She learns about kindness, compassion and sharing. One nagging question remains: is she good enough for a man like Griffin? Her father certainly doesn't think so....

Leap the Moon ...a Harlequin Superromance coming to you in August. Don't miss it!

LYNDA-1B